MYAL

MYAL

Erna Brodber

WAVELAND
PRESS, INC.
Long Grove, Illinois

For information about this book, contact:
Waveland Press, Inc.
4180 IL Route 83, Suite 101
Long Grove, IL 60047-9580
(847) 634-0081
info@waveland.com
www.waveland.com

Cover: *Nude in Thoughts,* © Paul Blackwood,
   http://www.paulblackwoodart.com/ab.php;
   email: prblackwood@hotmail.com; ph: 347-200-0606.

10-digit ISBN 1-4786-2311-X
13-digit ISBN 978-1-4786-2311-3

Printed in the United States of America

7 6 5 4 3

About the Author

Dr. Erna Brodber was born in deep, rural Jamaica, and after studying and working in Jamaica's major cities—Kingston and Montego Bay—as well as in several places in North America and Europe, she returned to live in Jamaica, becoming very involved in community work while writing fiction and nonfiction, including four novels, a collection of short stories, and one novel currently in press.

Trained in history and sociology, she also received a predoctoral fellowship in psychiatric anthropology. She worked in the Faculty of Social Science of the University of the West Indies as a lecturer and researcher from 1968 to 1985 when she returned to her natal village to work as an independent scholar. As such, she established Blackspace, an agency through which she encourages discussions on matters of relevance to the descendants of Africans enslaved in the New World.

Dr. Brodber has taught in many schools in the US, Canada, Europe, and several islands in the Caribbean. She has received several awards including the Gold Musgrave medal from the Institute of Jamaica for work in literature, another from the government of Jamaica for community work, and one from the government of the Netherlands for work in literature and orature.

She is the author of four novels: *Jane and Louisa Will Soon Come Home*, *Myal*, the winner of the Commonwealth Writers' Prize for Canada and the Caribbean, *Louisiana*, and *The Rainmaker's Mistake*, short-listed for the Commonwealth Writers' Prize for Canada and the Caribbean.

During the academic year 2013–2014, Dr. Brodber served as writer-in-residence in the Department of Literatures in English at the University of the West Indies, Mona.

ONE

Mass Cyrus said that it was not worms and that no black boil had broken in her either. He spoke very quietly. If those people had only learnt to deal with quietude and silence, they would have seen the notes on his score if not the dulce melodia – sweetly please –, the pp for soft, the diminuendo poco à poco – turn it down please –, and the curlicues for rest that Mass Cyrus face had become.

"These new people," his score was saying, "these in-between colours people, these trained-minded people play the percussions so loud and raucous, the wee small babe could know they feared the tune. Now, if they think of worms and black boil, why come to me? I am not that kind of doctor. No. They know it is something else, that only I can handle yet they come blasting my ears and shaking my etheric with their clashing cymbals. This discord could shake a man out of his roots.

"Another kind of people would have said: 'Mass Cyrus we need help.' Just that and shut up. In two two's the woman would be better. Curing the body is nothing. Touching the peace of those she must touch and those who must touch her is the hard part. And you can't do that unless you can touch their spirits. My people woulda humble them spirit and let me reach them: but this kind of people, . . . spirit too sekkle pekkle. Best let them keep their distance after all."
– Leave her here. An acre of land on a high hill. Bring the transfer paper with you when you come for her on Thursday, in six days time. –
The six days he wanted all to hear well. He wanted the woods and the trees, dry and green, growing and dying and the smallest stone bruise crawling in its many coloured fur to hear. They all knew no matter what their age or state that to get that grey mass out of that rigid, staring, silent female would take seven days and that she should be there until the end of the cure.

1

"Not so this time. The cure will not be completed in this grove. No matter what they say. A man has a right to protect his world. Woods and trees and stone bruise, you are right 90% of the time and I still need your strength but this needs 100%. I have to listen over your heads to the still small voice. It says this is the stinkest, dirtiest ball to come out of a body since creation and you can't handle it without their help. Let them take her away. On the seventh day it will pass from her but not in my grove. Oh no Siree. No Sir."

Nettie was shocked. In all her born days she had never felt such bitter vibrations coming from Mass Cyrus. Poor little thing. Inside her furry coat the thin strip of flesh that was her body trembled so violently that her feet, many though they were, could not hold the ground but skated her across the earth and under the dry trash and into the hollow at the root of the mango tree in search of friends and family. But although they all rushed to greet her and draped their little carpeted bodies over her or over those close to her in sympathy, the shaking did not cease but became a mighty hissing electric storm as she infected each little body with her tremors and each transmitted the infection to the other. Shook, shimmy and shake in the whole colony of stone bruise! Shook, shimmy and shake as they electrified the sap in the base of the mango tree so that its branches reared their heads and kicked their feet like so many wild jennies with no stockings to their can-can. Not even Mass Cyrus, who knew so many things, had realised before that young mangoes are metallic. The electric sap had tautened their bodies into tin and now in the mad orgasm of which they were a part, they shook their bells like Santa's sleigh. Whole lot of shaking going on! And the noise.

It was the noise that agitated those trees and shrubs that Mass Cyrus kept closest to his person – the bastard cedar, the physic nut and shy shame-mi-lady, mimosa pudica to you. On their shoulders he always placed the sin-generated afflictions of the human world. They felt it. The bastard cedar's eyes were quick to tears. One little hurt and its sap would flow right through the bark on to the side of the tree producing enough gum to fill a jam bottle and to seal a world of envelopes. And often times Mass Cyrus used these same tears turned to gum, to glue together a broken heart or a broken relationship until the organism could manage on its own again. This tree was by nature in a state of perpetual tension which is how come the slightest bruise by thought, word or deed sent its substance inside out. One wee electric mango grazed it and its high-strung self went gummy. The physic nut close by it began to bleed. And no wonder. With all the banging and ringing and splitting and weeping, it thought it was another good Friday many many years ago when the Saviour of the world was lynched. Every year it re-lived that occasion and its blood pressure would rise. Jab it and its life blood would come gushing out. Today, the noise made it particularly hypertensive and without help, it haemorrhaged. All this uncontrolled behaviour left shame-mi-lady embarrassed, so much so that her verdant train collapsed into a set of rigid lines like the railway tracks on a map only this time, green.

Mass Cyrus, sitting staring at the prostrate body of his patient, face in the cup of his palms, elbow on the weeping bastard cedar tree, listened to the cries and the hurts in his grove and he thought "This pain, confusion and destruction is what these new people bring to themselves and to this world." The thought hurt him in his very soul. From the soles of his feet to the tip of his head and it threw him upright and erect like a jack-in-a-box. Like Gonzalez with his statue of Marley, it yanked his head back, stiffened his right arm in front of him, pointed his index finger and glazed his eyes. Percy the chick uttered: "Lightning." And his spittle, a missile in a silver horn struck the line of coconut trees separating his grove from Jones' property. Slowly normalcy returned to the grove. Shame-mi-lady spread her wings like a peacock again, the crying and bleeding stopped, the mango tree resumed its old-man's posture of quiet meditation and if anyone had asked the little stone bruise what all that had been about, she would have opened her eyes wide and asked "What was all what about?" For curled up now like a satisfied cat at the base of the mango tree, she had forgotten and forgiven all.

The time was 1919. The lightning storm moved from Mass Cyrus' grove to adjacent districts of Manchioneal, Kensington and Hector's River and destroyed:

3

<pre>
71,488 coconut trees
 3,470 breadfruit trees
   901 residences totally
   203 residences partially
   628 out-buildings, and left
    65 standing but damaged.
</pre>

It killed 1,522 fowls, 115 pigs, 116 goats, five donkeys, one cow and one mule. Several humans lost their lives from drowning in the thunder storm and swollen rivers that it brought. So reported the Reverend Musgrave Simpson to his headquarters in Britain. All this sudden destruction because Ella O'Grady-Langley lying still like a grecian sacrifice upon a pyre had gone too far, had tripped out in foreign. "And they ain't seen nothing yet" Mass Cyrus smiled wryly. "What a bam-bam when that grey mass of muck comes out of this little Miss Ella lying down here so stiff and straight, this little cat choked on foreign, this alabaster baby, shipped on a banana boat and here to short circuit the whole of creation. But not in this grove though. A man has a right to protect his world. See how she shake up the whole place already." And he shook his head. For the trees and the buildings, which the freak storm which he drove from his grove destroyed, mostly belonged to his tribe of people. So did the lives. "What nigger for to do?" he sighed as many before him had done.

It was August 1919. Ella O'Grady-Langley was not fully twenty.

TWO

"Oh, where are you going to all you Big Steamers
With England's own coal, up and down the salt seas?"
"We are going to fetch you your bread and your butter
Your beef, pork, and mutton, apples and cheese"

"And where will you fetch it from, all you Big Steamers
And where shall I write you when you are away?"
"We fetch it from Melbourne, Quebec and Vancouver
Address us at Hobart, Hong Kong and Bombay"

"But if anything happens to all you Big Steamers
And suppose you are wrecked up and down the salt seas?"
"Why you'd have no coffee or bacon for breakfast
And you'd have no muffins or toast for your tea"

"Then I'll pray for fine weather for all you Big Steamers
For little blue billows and breezes so soft"
"Oh, billows and breezes don't bother Big Steamers
For we're iron below and steel rigging aloft."

The words were the words of Kipling but the voice was that of
Ella O'Grady aged 13. "Holness has scored with Getfield"
Reverend Simpson thought, as his eyes caught the smiling face
of the Anglican parson who was sitting in the visitor's chair
across from him. "Nice choice of poem what with the war about
to begin and all that. And well executed too." And his thoughts
went to the little lady executionist. She was doing very well. Very
well indeed. "Kipling" he said to himself as she settled into the
fifth verse:

"Then I'll build a new light house for all you Big Steamers
With plenty wise pilots to pilot you through"
"Oh the channel's as bright as a ballroom already,
And pilots are thicker than pilchards at Looe."

"There is another one" he said, as she mellowed, and like the second voice in a round, he kept pace with her, murmuring through her final verse:

Take up the whiteman's burden
Send forth the best ye breed
Go bind your sons to exile
To serve your captive's need
To wait in heavy harness
On filtered folk and wild
Your new caught sullen peoples
Half devil and half child.

The Reverend looked good at little Ella, sighed and said to himself: "And whose burden is this half black, half white child? These people certainly know how to make trouble." He looked around the school and continued with his conversation with himself: "No one else with that colour and that hair. You mean Holness couldn't have found another just as good? Seems we of this hue just cannot win!" No. He could have found no other. There was no one else in the school as sensitive as Ella O'Grady. No one else had reason to be.

The little girl had been born to Mary Riley from Ralston O'Grady, one of those Irish police officers whose presence the authorities must have felt, kept the natives from eating each other. As is usual, this new officer came to town with no wife and needed a housekeeper. As is also usual, the housekeeper was before long in the family way. What was unusual, was for said housekeeper to refuse to move to Kingston's anonymity to be kept by her baby-father and to opt to go back to her country bush of yam vines, coco roots and coconut trees. A big white man in a police officer's uniform would stick out a mile there. Poor pink O'Grady, dissonant as a skinned bull, didn't feel he could cope, so although he did have every desire to do right by Mary, things had to finish, done, end: they had was to part, my dear.

Those who always knew, knew that it shouldn't have end up that way. Mary should have did make the officer gentleman set her up and gone to Kingston with the stomach. But they mostly said it to themselves. Who dared to face her, talked, when it came, about the child and its future: "Mary you no see say this is a no nowhere fi bring up a little brown skin girl chile like that. If it was even a boy it coulda manage perhaps. But is a girl. The chile must study for nurse, or typist or something. You no see dis a no bush mout' pickney?" Mary paid these tongues no mind. She kept carrying the baby to the bush with her and as she grew bigger, to lean up her bunna on the root of a tree so that she could see all the things around her. When she could walk, she had her down there on the wharf with her. Such a well-behaved little girl! Ella just sat quietly laughing to herself in the big old hamper in which Mary left her while she carried her lot of bananas. Still people's mouth would not leave them. The sight of the mother and child vexed them. "Why this stupid ass woman have to carry this alabaster baby clear down pon the wharf? Mussa think is Moses and Miriam." Little Ella was in truth like an alabaster baby. The poor little pickney even had blue eyes which mercifully changed up to a more ordinary light brown as she grew. But the mouth and the skin and the hair didn't change much at all.

The whole strangeness of Mary and her child – looks and style – didn't just come from O'Grady and Mary's little time with him. Catherine Riley and Bada D did well strange too. Matter of fact, Bada D was strangeness itself. The man had thin lips, pointed nose and the hair thick and strong and curly like a coolie royal through Indian was nowhere in his strain for he step straight off of a African boat. That was common knowledge. Call himself a Moor. Said he came from Tanja and he was going back there. Mount Horeb was a hill where the man would sit for hours looking at the St. Thomas sea and dreaming about flying back to Africa. Who had patience with him? Everybody else want to go back and everybody else go back through the drums and the spirit; but that wasn't good enough for him. Bada D skin-up pon Kumina, join church and stick mongst them foolish people, bout them going send him back to minister to his people. Wouldn't even take a woman. Just spend time waiting. Then suddenly one day, he ups and marry Catherine Days, Miss Kate. Sickly woman. Same fine bone, thin lip kind of being. Must be he show her she was Moor too and that they could go hack home to Tanja together. So Catherine team up with Bada D. Smooth skin Catherine, colour barely turn. Something like tan tuddy potato. And out of them come Mary to make three long face, thin lip, pointed nose souls in a round face, thick lip, big eye country!

Whatever else grew in Catherine's delicate stomach went right back to the ground. So it was just the three of them by themselves. Bada D with his outlandish African self and his hoity hoity religion didn't exactly draw people to him like bees to honey, so the work in the ground had to be done mainly without neighbourly help and by the little band of three which really meant Mary and her father for the mother was delicate. Mary knew how to work hard. On top of that she was born to old people and was an only child so that she was accustomed to her own company. Even if people wanted her to help them waste time in chat and gossip, Mary just wouldn't know how to start. So she was this slender hard working girl, moving around swiftly and quietly like a self-contained majesty. Mrs. Holness didn't have to look far when Mrs. Repole came around asking for a "quiet girl from the country" to keep house for the new officer just come to work in Morant Bay.

Well, O'Grady liked her and kept her. Naturally. And could she jump around! For Mary housekeeping was doing the things she did at home. She was a farmer; she was house-wife; she was baker; she was seamstress. And so quiet. And on top of that she didn't object too strongly to giving O'Grady wife. Before long she was getting big. Mary went nowhere, Mary saw no one. Mary was a most upright woman. There was no other name to call. And Mary refused to go off to Kingston. The belly drew attention to O'Grady. He and it became the sign of misbehaving Irish policemen and O'Grady was transferred to where Mary knew not. So if she even wanted to go back on her stand and have the whiteman treat her and her child as quality, it could not now be done. So this was Mary now, though she told no one so or even thought it out straight: "that little thing on the bunna skin will simply have to find a way of dealing with the district people for I not going nowhere." And she became firmer when Miss Catherine followed Bada D to the grave and left her alone with the half acre of land. She was going to wrap that land close around her shoulders like a shawl till she dead and then they would sprinkle little bits of it upon her and say "Dust to Dust" and it would wrap her tight.

It was hard for Ella. It was hard for the district people. That Tanja dye, that could-be Moorish dye was light. No strength at all. It hardly showed in her. The whiteman didn't have to give her fine skin, straight nose, thin lips and growing hair for she already got that from the Riley side. He could only give her the colour and a little straightening on the hair to make her look white and that is what he gave her. And the skin so sensitive! It was a rebuke to the very elements. Two little ants just bite her and the hand swell up like somebody beat her. No pleasure to fight with. The skin would show every craab you give her and you woulda feel bad. When you fighting a girl, you must lick her down and hold on to the plaits where the mother separate each clump of hair from the other, and shake the head until you feel the scalp lift from the skull. You coulda do that with Ella? That chile hair have only two sections. One path down the centre of her head with just two plaits hanging down. They themselves begin at the child's ears. Where you going to get clump of hair near the scalp to shake? You can fight with that?

So the children only said she was raw and more so when rain fall and wouldn't deal with her at all. The most they would do is scream out "Salt pork", "Alabaster baby", "Red Ants Abundance" when they saw her. When teacher taught the whole school the game "O'Grady says", he never thought he was giving them something new with which to beat the child. And when the new dance came down from Kingston:

> Mrs. O'Grady, she was a lady
> Who had a daughter
> Whom I adore
> And every evening
> I used to court her
> I mean the daughter
> Every Sunday, Monday,
> Tuesday, Wednesday, Thursday
> Friday, Saturday
> At half past four.
> She was tall
> And slim

9

> And her hair
> Was a delicate shade of ginger,

Ella became "ginger". She was tall and slim and her hair was "a delicate shade of ginger". They knew nothing about hair being shades of ginger but they did know that ginger was for belly-ache and was harsh. Nothing nice in that. And there was worse: I used to "court" her. "Courten". Slack, you couldn't say a word like that around big people. So they didn't say it, but Ella and everybody knew that when they shouted out "Ginger" and sniggered they were really accusing her of doing a very dirty thing, every Sunday, Monday, Tuesday, Wednesday, Thursday, Friday, Saturday at half past four.

Then the rumour started that Ella had lice and with all that hair the mother couldn't get to treat it. Which was true but no more so than for the others for everyone had lice now and again. And Mary was working on it. It was precisely because someone saw her buying Cooper's Dip with which to treat the hair, that the rumour started. The child already had a corner seat in her class at school. Now anybody who had to sit on the one side of her, squinge themselves up to leave a space between them and she. Say them don't want to get the lice that probably in their own heads long time! So Ella made the door to the class room her recess spot. She would go no further than the door when teacher let the class out. Not a step further. Funny her two foot didn't wear out from years of standing on the concrete during recess, year in year out.

The teachers didn't too warm to her either so she couldn't stay behind with them and clean the blackboard or help to tidy up or any little thing like that. She could only stand at the door and stare into space and they said "That child is odd. No fight at all. Suppose the colour will carry her through." And they were more than a little vexed at that and built up resentment against her. For it was true. With all the books they had read and exams they had sat around trying to pass, and the men they couldn't enjoy because they might disgrace the profession, no one was going to give them with their black selves any job as a clerk anywhere in Kingston or Morant Bay or any other town anywhere in the world. It didn't make any sense beating out themselves on this child and having the embarrassment of seeing welts on her from the slightest touch of the strap, when she was going to get through anyhow. So they stopped seeing her and she too stopped seeing them.

They didn't bother to ask her anything in class. She found a way to learn though. Her mother used to tell her that the angels would keep her and teach her many things and perhaps that's what happened. In a science class, teacher would talk about OSMOSIS, "the process by which a thin substance pulls a thick substance through a thin cell wall". Miss Prince would ask who knew what osmosis was and Ella would put up her hand but never be called on. Perhaps teacher wanted to find somebody who didn't know so that she could beat it into his head. Once more unrecognized, Ella would stare through the windows and guess what? She would see the thin liquid struggling to pull the thick one and all of this within the membrane of a little leaf. Like an object lesson. And so everytime. When they brought out the maps and showed Europe, it rose from the paper in three dimensions, grew big, came right down to her seat and allowed her to walk on it, feel its snow, invited her to look deep down into its fjords and dykes. She met people who looked like her. She met Peter Pan and she met the Dairy Maid who could pass for her sister – same two long plaits and brownish. She met the fellow with the strange name who put his finger in the dyke and stopped the town from flooding. Funny, she never met O'Grady in all her travels. Ella wasn't sad about that. She didn't think she would like him.

So when Teacher brought his poem about Steamers, he wasn't bringing any new idea to Ella except for the part about getting up and reciting before the whole school. She had been to England several times. To Scotland too and had watched them playing the bagpipes. She liked that. Liked to see the little tassel moving on the men's hats and their skirts gently caressing their rear as they moved like one man forward blowing through those leather bags so easily. Peter had taken her into a coal mine and up through a chimney and she had come out looking more like her mother. She remembered that trip very well for it was the first time she felt real but then they had walked along the streets and people had teased them

11

and said "Look at the little blackamoors" and she didn't like it because she didn't think a person's colour was anything to make a joke about. Often they had gone down to Cardiff, the place where there were so many ships and she and Peter, and Lucy Gray who was now part of their party, had spoken to the ships big and little and asked them the very same questions that were in Teacher's poem. But they were luckier than the children in this recitation for they had taken them with them and they had seen Quebec and Vancouver and all those places and could see the channel for themselves and the cargo that the ships were taking on. It was nothing, nothing at all. All she was doing at Teacher's rehearsals was to open her mouth and let what was already in her heart and her head come out.

Teacher Holness' face was a mixture of gladness and stale amazement. "Not even Anita could do that," he was thinking as he watched the child. "How can that child sit so quietly on all that talent? No one had the slightest suspicion of its existence! Strange child" he concluded, still amazed.

THREE

This was the time of day that Maydene liked. The gloaming. No. Twilight. Not that. The dusk. No. Nightfall. Yes. The right word at last. That was Maydene. The effort to be true to any place or situation that she found herself in. If she were in the British Isles, the time of day that meant so much to her would have been called the "gloaming" but she was in St. Thomas, Jamaica. Nightfall then. The right word. But there was something still missing. For it wasn't just the fall of the night that was hers. It was the "cusp". Her personal word. She said it under her breath. "Cusp". "Cusp" was a word that delighted her from the day they met. "A point where two curves meet," the dictionary had said. That was what she liked about the time called nightfall. The meeting of two disparate points. Then, she felt that she was at the beginning of a new phase of creation. Felt as if God particularly wanted her to watch Him change scenes. A great honour and a continuing pleasure. And the drama, the pleasure and the honour were more intense in St. Thomas than any other place she had been. The day could be bright yellow right up to the change and then night would fall, literally like a black curtain. Life changed too. The peeny wally winked around, the frogs came out hop-hopping, the owl entered centre stage and the whistling toads and crickets made background music throughout the play. Most folks closed their doors then, and only the beam of pale yellow light which escaped through the chinks of their wattle houses told you that they were alive. All God-fearing folks turned in out of respect, shyness or fear, while God made His changes. Except Maydene Brassington, the wife of the Methodist minister in charge of the parish of St. Thomas. People didn't know what to make of her. If she were of their tribe, they would say that she was dealing in darkness or that like Miss Gatha, she could see. But the lady was lily white, English and high. Mrs. Reverend William Brassington. They dismissed her as strange.

13

It was no surprise to Smith that his mistress should tell him a couple minutes after they had left Grove Town School and the breaking up, that he should leave her there to find her way home and take the opportunity of having Taylor look at the horse's hoof. When night was about to fall, it was one excuse or another. The buggy did need some overhauling and Taylor did live in that district. But Smith was not fooled. The lady just wanted to do whatever she did at that time of the day. But he was wrong this time. It was not the desire to watch God create that made Maydene dismiss her coachman and prepare to walk the three miles into Morant Bay when dusk was turning into night. Maydene wanted to meditate and in Grove Town.

"Now" she began in her head, "William and this place. They have an unhealthy relationship. And that is bad for him." Maydene saw herself as the monitor of her husband's soul. "The whole parish of St. Thomas is his," she continued, "and true, he cannot see to every little corner of it especially when he also has to supervise the young clerics in the whole county of Surrey. True, there is a kind of unwritten agreement that each of the denominations should have a particular sphere of influence within the parish and true the Baptists and the Anglicans already have a strong presence here. But William has not tried." Like Mr. Dombey's sister of Dickensian fame, Maydene believed in trying. And applied it to herself also. She would try with William's problem until she dropped. She continued analysing him. "Take today for instance. The excuse he gave for not attending this little function is that he has to visit two or three of his out-stations. Plausible. But the relief at having an excuse was too great. Too much energy is put into this avoidance."

And she walked along, intense as usual, digging so deeply into William's head, that she heard no toads, saw no frogs, the crickets chirped to themselves and if God was waiting for applause for making the night out of thick black felt, He would have to turn to somebody else. And she continued, rehashing arguments word for word. "William," I have said: "You are neglecting the people right at your door step who might want to join the Methodist fellowship." And he has said everytime: "May, you don't know. Let me work where I can

14

get results. I would need a sledge hammer to move Grove Town." I have suggested all sorts of things. An open air meeting. A good suggestion I still think but he has said to everything: "It wouldn't help. Let Getfield or whatever home man the Anglicans send, minister there. They don't know what Grove Town is so it doesn't seriously matter what they do. The Baptists are doing well. Let them continue. Simpson. Good worker. That nobody can deny but a bit too hard for me to take."

Maydene found this Baptist parson quite a reasonable man. But a clear message came from her husband that he would prefer if she kept him at a distance. She rolled her husband's insides around in the palms of her hands like Cook making dumplings, searching for the not-yet smooth side. "What is it?" William was a very rational man, usually, and from the earliest days they had always discussed issues both of a public and a private nature fully and frankly with each other but Grove Town and the Rev. Simpson were a different kettle of fish. It bothered Maydene that William's bother was so deep-set that he feared to let it surface, and if it didn't, how was she to help him as she ought? It bothered her that it was something very simple and that any woman born in Jamaica would have been able to fathom it, in which case, the mirror was showing a clash, not a joining of cultures and there went one mark against her marriage and a telling blow to her faith in the intrinsic beauty in the meeting of unlikes. The bother bothered her continually.

Listening to that little girl and watching her as she recited was what set Maydene to thinking of William and his bother. Funny. In the middle of that child's recitation, she ceased to see her and saw William instead. There was good reason. William was of the same kind of mixture as this girl. That was one of the first things William told her about. Innocent and beautiful, just like that little girl, he had faced the congregation that Sunday at Linton as a student at Cambridge. Her father had been impressed by his erudition and his exoticism and invited him to tea. It was the strength of his spirit, its beauty and passion that had attracted her. Right away he told them of his origins. An invisible mother. Possibly half caste. Very like the kept woman of somebody important.

She had died giving birth to him. He had been cared for, after age ten by a large settlement from his father whom he did not know; had been brought up by a negress supervised by a Methodist minister, now dead, and by his father's very worthy attorney who saw to his financial needs.

Maydene's mind went back to that day in Linton and then on to her father. "Father was a strange man. Still is," she reflected. "That William was not all white was as important to him as to William but with different values. Where William was apologetic, Father was delighted. He literally rubbed his hands in glee and though he did not actually say them, the words were in his eyes: 'Ah, I've caught a fish alive.' He talked that day and many after, about the greatness of Pushkin and Beethoven. He claimed that they were men of colour and attributed their greatness to genes. William by inference was either great or going to be great. In an age when every other country parson felt that his true calling was the scientific study of man, Father was in the front line of the new thinking – all by himself."

"All people were of one brown colour but some cataclysmic occurrence had brought ice to some parts of the earth and heat to others, made some people black, others white and created different systems of behaviour. He expected that some other such event would return the world to its former state. It was the mixture of black and white that would be most attuned to the new setting. And he would bore everyone with his rhetorical questions 'When you cross oxygen and hydrogen, don't you get something different from both and uniquely necessary to man – water?' 'Have you noticed how well they do in spite of the world's prejudices against them? Wasn't it the brown Simon of Cyrene who carried the Christ's cross?' Perhaps because no-one ever took his theories seriously, Father thought he was a second Noah. He was enthralled by this man with a touch of black. Mother of course had him thoroughly investigated when she realized that my interest in him was not a show to humour Father, nor a flirtation with the exotic. She was delighted to whisper that there was nobility somewhere. Some very very important person used to go to the Tropics for the winter, had had a secret situation there and left a seed behind. No names had been given but there was William's inheritance to prove it. I only wanted to understand that passion." This last she said aloud and then continued her silent soliloquy.

"He must have grown up like that little girl. One strange face in a sea of colour. Lonely among his own people. But that couldn't be it: All his stations, as Grove Town would be, are full of black faces." She returned to the little girl. There was something else, she thought that she had, that William had that day he came to Linton. "That little girl looked as if she was flying. Totally separated from the platform and from the people around her. Not just by colour but as an angel in those Sunday school cards is separated from the people below. Swimming in the sky, or flying or whatever, in that ethereal fashion over all below. It is that." She said to herself. "It is that angelic look that I saw, its root in a passion so innocent and strong that it could separate body from soul. Funny, Father and I really saw the same thing. We both saw the abstract. I called it passionate innocence, he called it the spirit of the new age." And she went back to the little girl, "But she is not happy up there in the sky. She wants to be real. Is that it? Does William want to be real? Has he become real and doesn't like it?" The questions were like ribbons of different colours on a maypole and Maydene saw that they were about to tangle. She must stop now. "Whatever is William's bother is tied up with reality, that little girl and Grove Town and I can do no more tonight." She quit, deciding to let her mind lie fallow and to let the elements from the atmosphere come in and do what ordering they could.

The toads, the peeny wally, the crickets and all the night creatures were alive again, hissing, singing, gurgling, whistling. They joined the crush of hard leather on gravel – Maydene's shoes. And she heard another sound which she hadn't heard in a long time. The bup-bup of Miss Gatha's bare foot on gravel, domineering the stones into the very earth. She picked up the scent of an elderly female. Maydene knew she was right. What other female would be walking in the night besides her? She loved her and felt that she was loved. They never ever spoke but neither needed words to know that each was happy that the other existed. Miss Gatha passed her in silence. The night was too black for Maydene to see her but she knew that a pair of feet each with its five strong and very black toes swung the skirt of her long multi-coloured dress, that her collar held closely to her neck, that her head-wrap cut across her ears, plain at the top with the cloth folded at the back into antennae. And the big wooden wheels rocked in her ears.

Maydene smiled to herself "I wouldn't like to walk barefooted but I would like to wear that head-dress." Then she laughed aloud: "My straight hair wouldn't give it half a chance to stay on. That's the point," she said "William will not laugh or even allow me to laugh at such things. He would want Miss Gatha to give up her head-dress and put on my hat and be very grieved if she refused to. That is it. In church after church, the colourful clothes have gone, replaced by colour-less white and those felt hats which people buy – buy you know – and wear only on Sundays. What an expense when a head tie could be made to serve all occasions and later when too worn, be cut to make clothes for a grandchild! Why does William do these things? And why do people allow him to get away with it. 'Don't you wear a hat to church? Why should my people not wear hats? Isn't it nice that all of us in the fellowship behave in the same way?' What do you do with that? I have warned him. 'William' I have asked, 'Have you got what to give people instead when you take away what they've got?' 'William' I have said, 'You are a thief' and then he jokes, 'Your hat or their clothes?' 'William, you are a spirit thief. You keep taking away these people's spirit. Remember the cleansed man into whom seven devils more powerful than the first entered?' 'But your hat my dear will hold them' and I had laughed so much. But he had continued more seriously 'That is the nature of this kind of ministry – to exorcise and replace'."

Maydene paused. She had never truly seen herself before from William's point of view. "I don't think I like at all being held up as the thing with which to fill those sacks which he has emptied. I don't approve at all. I see old men who must know by now how to live their lives, sitting empty in church, unable to read the responses, just waiting for the word that comes out of William's mouth. I wouldn't like that power. He has reduced them to children. Much better if he could find a way of linking what they know with what he wants them to know. They wouldn't seem so inadequate. He says it's a stage of conversion that all new Christians have to pass through. Was Father's ministry like that? He gave advice and he preached the word and he counselled. I suppose his business was really to brace the already converted. I do pray that William can as he thinks he can, refill those people." Maydene smiled at the thought of Miss Gatha. "No way he could take away her head-dress" and congratulated her silently. "So that is it!" She felt she now held the germ. "That is why he would need a sledge hammer. Grove Town people would resist his efforts to separate them from their understanding of life. But he doesn't even try which is strange for William," she said.

Around the corner, she saw the lights of her own house and could see from the shadow cast through the glass windows that William was home and that he had pulled back a corner of the curtain and was watching for her return. "Poor dear," she said involuntarily, empathising with the child in her husband that needed her so, then consciously, as she saw what she had learnt, "Poor dear. William is crippled by the fear of going back to the Grove Town of his past. We never ever discussed those early years though I have read this man Freud." That the little girl was going to help her, Maydene resolved. "She will be my daughter. After all, I have always wanted to have a daughter."

FOUR

All Mrs. Brassington said to Cook was that she would like to know the mother of the light-skinned girl with the long brown hair who recited so well at the function on Sunday at Grove Town School. Thereupon, Cook complained to Coachman that she did not know what she could teach Mary's soft-skin scattered-brained child whom Mrs. Brassington was going to apprentice to her. From there the news winked about and settled into Mrs. Amy Holness' kitchen. Miss Jo usually carries water for her and it was she who asked her that morning if she had heard that the white lady who was the methodist parson's wife was going to take Mary's strange girl as a schoolgirl. That set Mrs. Holness head hurting with vexation that she couldn't express. Those people were coming to her once again to ask her to get Mary Riley to give up her all. A little air and a little rocking might help and as she passed through the pantry, through to the dining room and the drawing room and on to the verandah, one little curse word formed in her head: blast. There were more. She would rock them out of her head. That would relieve the pressure that was building up in there.

You could call her a prophet for she had hardly let herself down into the rocking-chair before she saw Maydene Brassington making her way pass the almond tree, close to the spot where one path leads to the school and the other to the teacher's cottage. Amy knew she was right. She was taking the left turn. She was coming to her, not to her husband at school and the cursing began to circle in her head: "This blasted white pillow case with a string tied in the middle. These white people just wan tek people pickney fi practice pon. Want Mary good-good pickney fi pasture out to her two red-face son. Is pumpkin belly dem wan send this one back home with too?" But since Amy Holness was the headmaster's wife and Maydene Brassington the parson's wife, there was no way what was in her head could be expressed in that way.

20

It stayed there circling. Instead, she said when Maydene began to ascend her steps: "Why Mrs. Brassington how nice to see you. What a coincidence! Someone just called your name to me. They say you are wanting to take Mary's child into your house." She did not wait for a response. "A real coincidence", she continued. "Her mother saw service for a little time you know. With an officer in Morant Bay. I was the one who made the contact for him through a Mrs. Repole. Do you know her?" The pause was too short for an answer. Amy Holness continued "My, your boys will love her. She will fit so well into the family. They are expected home soon, aren't they? Such lovely gentlemen!"

Maydene Brassington was not fooled by the translation. She knew that Mrs. Holness was saying "You interfering white slob. Why don't you go and do your dirty work yourself and leave me to my business?" "And that's another thing", she thought, "that William refuses to deal with. That there are classes everywhere and that those below must hate those above and must devise some way of communicating this without seeming too obviously rude. He refuses to participate in 'silly linguistic rituals'. 'Humility', he would say, 'Humility . . . My people have a far way to go and a far way we can go but we must understand how far back we are and submit so that we can learn. Come out with it and be done'. He would come home grumbling about how long it took to get through a meeting because of linguistic rituals. But this is a part of life everywhere. Why expect anything different here? Just William once more wanting people to empty themselves in front of him so that he can remodel them into shapes of which he approves." Maydene was in no hurry to go. She had got her foot into one Grove Town house and she was not going to miss this chance to breathe in its essence, savour it, analyse it and co-exist with it. Nothing that God made was going to frighten her. So if Mrs. Holness thought that just because she was black, was a couple rungs below her socially, she could roll this into a weapon with which to distance her, she would have to think again.

Maydene settled in and tried to look comfortable on the little bentwood chair handed her, though to tell the truth her fat hips were drooping over the sides like a Friday evening hamper on a donkey's back. She knew how ridiculous she looked and she knew how uncomfortable she felt, but she peeped into the drawing room and admired the ruffles and the tatting on the centre table aloud and said to herself, above her discomfiture, "She doesn't know it yet, but we are going to be friends and she is going to teach me to make all those delicious things they make with coconuts". Then she proceeded to smile into space. Her silence was off-putting. Amy had no more leads. She simply had to wait until Maydene chose to toss the ball back to her. And Maydene pushed her advantage even further to dictate the level and the tone of the conversation. The matter on the floor was of course the exploitation of people's natural god-given gifts – their selves or those of the beings they made. Amy had accused her of stealing her people and exploiting their bodies.

The accusation was too oblique to force a direct response. Maydene would side step that, take another tack and throw her slightly. She looked at the floor which was incredibly shine. It truly was a marvel to her how these people managed to get and to keep their floor so shine. – Mrs. Holness – she said – How do you manage to grow up children and keep your floor so shine? – She did know that Mrs. Holness had no children. Amy broke.

– Teacher and I really have no children you know – and that was more of a truth than Maydene wanted or even knew she got or Amy knew she had let out, for she had one by somebody else and that Teacher was supporting Michael, though she had given him none of his own, was a constant source of distress.

– But I bet there is a special one you wish was yours. –

– Yes – and Amy's eyes went soft.

– There is. – And she went into hymns of praise about Anita, how bright she was, how Teacher was hoping that she would go off to somewhere where she could make something of her life; how she didn't quite like the life she was living – her mother left her too often alone and went off to Town; how people were really very strange and you can't very well ask them to give over their children to you though you think you could do a better job; how she would simply have to wait until Miss Euphemia – the mother – felt that she would take good

care of the child and not treat her as a maid. But that was life.
– Yes – Maydene said, – That is life indeed. – The argument
had come to where she wanted, quicker than she had dared
to hope.
– You know then that I understand that you must hesitate
about the little girl that you know I have come about. –
– You see Mrs. Brassington – Amy was no longer on her high
linguistic horse. She had gone back into her real self and
about seventeen years before – People look around and see
children living with people who are not their parents and
think that it is easy for us to part with our child, I mean
children, – she back-tracked to cover her slip. – But it is not
easy. And I hate to see how circumstances can force people
to give their children to others. So I know that I would be
asking a big thing of Miss Euphemia. Now you, I don't know
how you see these matters. You have children but they are
not with you. You know how many people tried to get Mary
Riley to leave here with her child? She stayed here and
together they bore a lot and I have a great deal of respect
for that effort. I don't know how to see what you are asking.
To tell you the truth I am not sure that I know what you are
asking. –
     One truth deserves some others and Maydene admitted it.
– That's true. I really don't know what I want. I can say though
that I am not looking for a maid. Cook is quite competent.
You should know though that I fell in love with the little girl
that day when I saw her reciting. You do know that my
husband is Jamaican. – Amy knew she meant 'not full white'
and at another time would have feigned surprise, "But Mrs.
Brassington, how extraordinary." Today she was silent and
Maydene went on. – There are things about him that I
therefore cannot easily understand. When I saw that child, I
saw him. You don't need to tell me that that child's colour
makes her uncomfortable in a district like this. That much I
can see. What I am only now beginning to see is the
enormous size of the pain my husband must have lived
through as a child. That doesn't tell you what I am asking. I
know that. – And she too was silent. There on the little
verandah, Adam and Eve looked away from each other for
they had eaten the forbidden fruit. Maydene had nothing else

23

to say, so she said – That's all I can say. – To which Amy replied, – I'll take you to see Mary. –

Who was not there and Amy should have known. It was a weekday morning and at a time like this when all the planting had been done – and it didn't take Mary long to cover a little half acre ground –, Mary would have long gone to the property to head bananas. Or she would have betaken herself down to the wharf a couple miles away to head them not from the field to the cart this time, but from the railway station to the wharf. – I don't suppose you can come on a Sunday or a Saturday. I know that a parson's wife is extra busy on those days, – Amy said, – so come back in the evening of one of the weekdays. I will get a message around to Mary that you are trying to see her. I won't make any promises but it is possible that she might want to come to see you to find out what it is. – They were back to linguistic ritual and they knew it. This was life. They both knew that the visit of the teacher's wife and the parson's wife meant that poor Mary when she heard of it was duty bound to make her way as fast as she could to find out what they had wanted. Mary was strange and strong-willed. But not as strange and as strong-willed as that. And there was no need to send her any message either. By now the news would have reached her that Miss Amy had taken the Methodist parson's wife to see her and even from the distance she was, people would be asking her what they had come about, as if by their very presence at her house some silent communication had been established. Amy Holness' nonsensical comment was just something to break the silence. Something like 'Good Evening'. A kind of prelude to it as they walked to the Cross Roads.

Maydene thought of William's reaction to her visit. She didn't need to tell him either. He too would hear of it through the grapevine and know of it even before he reached home this evening. Maydene Brassington walking about in the parish was not news: parson's wife just liked to walk around quietly by herself and more so at nightfall. But a white woman and a black woman walking together quietly and comfortably like equals was news. It would be an incident which people used to mark events. By the time William reached the outskirts of Morant Bay, someone would have said to him. "So Parson, you trying with Grove Town now", meaning "Your Missus went up there today. Did you send her to feel out the possibilities of setting up a mission station there?" Or someone else would have said more pointedly "Parson how nice of you to send the Missus into Grove Town to minister to the sick," which would have meant, "Your wife with her busybody self has gone up to Grove Town and has been there mixing with those kinds of people". If William wasn't too tired he would see the expression on their faces which gave the true message and be annoyed with 'linguistic ritualism'. If he was very tired, he would only hear and see that Maydene had gone to Grove Town. Whatever the message and whatever the state of his being, Maydene knew she would have to explain. At the thought of finding an explanation for William, she remembered Amy's implied question-accusation and felt ready to respond.

– The boys – she said – My boys. They are at school in England. But you already know that. Why? They were born there, spent some years here and are back there for secondary training. I could say that I have a lot of work to do and couldn't manage the raising of them too, but that wouldn't be quite true because if I had to, I would. By the way, it might not look so to you but I do have a lot of work to do. One day we must talk about that. – In her forthright way, as simple as the clothes she wore, Maydene continued: – Mrs. Holness, it is not a pleasant thing to admit to a poor black person, but the fact is that certain people have become accustomed to certain styles of life and since they have the money to continue it, they do. That as honestly as I can give it to you, is why the boys are at school in Britain. One problem with that is that there is so much about Jamaica, which will quite likely be their home, that they do not know. And please, do not worry, Ella will not be helping them to know Jamaican women. True, they are 15 and 17 and might want to. I don't think they are like that. At any rate, I hope they are not like that. Very feeble. A very feeble statement. A very feeble assurance, I know. But I have seen their father's suffering and know now that I have only seen the tip of it. I would protect the child. We are being a bit previous aren't we? But yes, it is a matter I must study. –

Miss Amy by now had forgotten the question and was convinced that Ella should go with Mrs. Brassington. So many girls were dying for a place where they could learn a couple of skills with which to make a living. She was now 13. Two more years in school. She wasn't bright. Definitely wasn't bright. And was strange. More, people still didn't know what to do with her. That recitation was just chance. She had done very well and brought honour and attention to herself and to Jacob. But how many more inspection days were there left for her to recite? Two more. Thirteen and still in fourth book. Never even a skip! Nobody to pay for extra lessons for her. There was really nothing for her to do in this district and to tell the truth she really don't look good carrying basket on her head. When Mary called she would put certain truths to her. Even if Mrs. Brassington was to take her just as a schoolgirl that would be good but she would tell Mary that there were even better possibilities for her and hope that if she decided to deal with Mrs. Brassington, she would bargain for something like a typist's course. With her hair and colour she could get far. And no point stopping in her way. Who knows, the child might even remember her mother and give her a little help. If Mrs. Brassington wanted to do what O'Grady didn't do, then that too was just life. You never know who is going to set the balance right.

Once somebody started giving out some goodness, you didn't know who wouldn't get. A sewing machine might come for Michael; Euphemia might give them Anita and stop her feeling so guilty that Jacob was supporting her child closeted at her parents' house. Life was strange.

That night she dreamt that she was at the edge of a beautiful river. She was alone on her side and on the other side were all her friends and family. It was as if there was a picnic planned for their side of the river but she had lost her way and ended up on the wrong side. They were all happy to see her and were waving their hats and shouting to her to come over. She could see no path. Only the clear river beside her, so clear that she could see the river stones in it. Nobody had disturbed that water for a long time. It was very clear and clean. It was not the kind that one washed in for there was no tell-tale sign of any bit of cloth or old garment close by. It was not a river to fish in because

26

there was no sign of any janga or shrimps running in it. Even the stones were strange. Normally they were cream coloured and soft looking in that area so you knew that if you stepped in, the water might become cloudy as your feet rubbed the sediment from the stones. These were not like that. These were hard stones and cemented together so that if your feet should touch them you would find a solid uniform surface. The trouble was though, that her feet could not reach the security of the stones. She would have to swim. And the others kept saying "Just swim over. It is easy."

There was something about the dream that she didn't like for there were some dead over on the other bank side along with the living. But the clean water was a good sign. Jacob agreed. It certainly was a mixed up dream but he too felt that the clean water was a good sign. Teasingly he said to her "You can swim it. Just stretch out your feet and kick. In less than no time you over the river with them. But see that you carry me on your back." He felt it had something to do with the Brassingtons. When Amy had told him of Mrs. Brassington's visit, he had seen hope. "Look like something might break Amy" was what he said. He felt that the dream was a confirmation of his diagnosis. He had worked so hard to up the grade of the school. Look at the effort to find a poem which taught History, Geography and Civics! And better still, love for the Empire, so badly needed with England facing war. Fourteen years in one school and no invitation to a higher grade was nothing to be proud of.

FIVE

Anita was studying. The kind that splits the mind from the body and both from the soul and leaves each open to infiltration. She was solfa-ing. This took a lot of concentration. She had to read the notes – first note on the line is "e" – and she had to remember the sounds. "Do re mi fa so la ti do." So if that was "e", it was really "mi" and she sounded it. Now that next one is the first space so it has to be "f" and if it is "f" coming after "e" then it must be "fa" and she sounded that. Then she went back: "Do re mi fa." So what she really wanted was "mi, fa" and she sounded those two. "Mi fa." The other one was a little bit more difficult. It was all the way to the end: the last note on the line so it had to be "f". Now to get at that sound. "Do re mi fa so la ti do." So that was "do". So the three first notes in the piece were "mi fa do". Now to sing them. And she got it. "Mi fa do." Now the words: "Thee I love." She had got it. Now to press on a little further. Teacher had said it was easy. Other sounds joined hers. She heard a slight "ping" but she continued to the fourth note. Now this one was three spaces below the first line and had a short line through it. And in her mind she reversed. "E" is the first note on the line, "d" had to be the first note below the line, so the one close to it with the line through it, has to be "c". She had pictured that. Now she had to sound it. She reversed the sound. "E" was "mi", "d" was "re", so that had to be "do". So it was now "mi fa do do" and this last "do" was a deep one. So she sang "mi fa do. Do–". Now the words: "Thee I love. More . . ." Ping. Another one that!

It wasn't the sound of the zinc expanding on the roof. That was not usually half as sharp and it tended to move "Dup dup dup". In any case it was now evening and there was no sun to cause it to expand. Ping. Sharp and stronger this time. "Is who throwing stone on the house at this time of the evening?" she called out. "You boys stop it." And she went out to pose with her beautiful fifteen-year-old body for though she was very very bright in academic matters and knew it, she also knew that she had a nice skin and a nice shape and that the boys were always trying to get her attention. She opened the door to make her stage appearance when "ping", it caught her right in the middle of her forehead and she saw the little white pebble drop. "You know you lick me?" she shouted. And another "ping" sounded on the zinc. But Anita was not going to move. She was big and bad. "Lick me again if you think you bad." "Thud." It hit her this time on her collar-bone. "But what is this though, you know you lick me?" And this time she closed the door. "You just wait til my mother come." But the stones continued to rain on the house. And even when it got quite dark! Anita wondered what boys it could be. Who was going to be sitting in one place throwing stones for hours and not come out to boast? That is if is even a boy or some boys! But what else could it be?

Her mother said that it must be the boys and she must tell Teacher about it next day. Euphemia really thought "That must be one persistent fellow!" But she didn't want to give that thought air, for she was too tired. She had been way up in the hills nearly to go to Hardwar Gap looking skellion to make up her load to go to the Princess Street market. She would have to get up early, hand up the bananas, make them drain a little, wrap up the yampie in banana trash, grease the measuring cans and get change. She must run round to Taylor and see if he can make some change for her. Taylor. Then she remembered that things had changed. Wasn't quite sure that she should run to Taylor, but who else? She hadn't worked out that yet. Must get some sleep for Mass Levi was coming early and he could only drop her at Whitehorses; she would have to walk fast and see if she could catch Mass Cephas at Yallahs if she wanted to get into Town tomorrow to make anything out of the Friday market. So much to do before Mass Levi reached! No time to think bout stone pon house top. Wasn't her house. She was only renting it. People want mash up the roof, Mass Levi business that. Him will have to repair it. Yes. She would tell him about how the boys throwing stone on the house and let him look bout that. The other thing was that she didn't want to think about Anita and boys. She knew how she had been at that age. Tease out them life! But Anita's head was always in some book! She had hoped that she wasn't going to bother with that just now. And she was alone in the house so often. Plenty she could do if she want to be bad. She would let that be and hope. Talk to Mass Levi about it tomorrow and let Anita talk to Teacher.

Anita was no longer a schoolchild. She had passed fifteen some months now and her age was up in school. But Teacher kept her on as a monitor and he was hoping that the school had done so well at the inspection that the inspector and the board would recommend that he be given some money for a pupil teacher and then he would hire Anita and let her have a little pocket money to help herself. Right now, she was helping out with A class and he would find some time during the day to help her learn some extra things. She could still come to the evening classes and she did. But there was really nothing more there for her to learn as she had already at age 15 passed the preliminary examinations one, two and three. She was too young to go to college and in any case where was the money for that? So he would just teach her a few new things and if she caught on, he would even let her sit the Pupil Teachers' exams. If they resisted her because of her age, he would just get him the exam papers after the sitting and let her do a kind of mock exam. That would keep her in good form when the right time came. Last night he had taught her the rudiments of music. She was quick there too and what a nice voice she had! Not strong but sweet. Carried a melody nicely.

Anita's head had grown a quite observable coco. Teacher made the connection right away between the stone throwing she had told him about and it. He would whip every child in the school until he found out who had done it. He wasn't a man given to much violence but people must learn to treasure what is good and particularly when it is their own. "Look at this child, a tribute to the whole of Grove Town and someone fling stone and lick her in her head like that? Suppose it was the eye? Every day they hear it. 'Don't throw stones. Stones have no eyes, they cannot see.' But they wouldn't hear." But there was no confession. Nobody had seen anyone and nobody had heard of anything from anyone. At lunchtime he asked Amy what she thought. It was only then that he saw Anita as more than brains. Amy had laughingly suggested that some young man might be trying to get Anita's attention. It was then that he saw the smooth black skin, the high chest, the sink in her back and the spread of her buttocks; saw her win that race as she did everything else and saw himself thinking as he had done then, "What a fine, well-groomed horse." He felt foolish. "Fancy beating practically the whole school for that! Amy we must take that child immediately. Too much work gone into her for some stupid district boy to take her and send her with yam to market. Now. Now. Such a high-spirited girl. So sure of herself. And that laugh when she has learnt something new. Pity the poor fellow. He can't match her. Can only throw stones on her house top."

Whoever wanted to gain Anita's attention took a very long time to reveal himself. The stones continued to fall every evening that God sent. The little zinc-roofed house became a public spectacle. People were coming from Morant Bay and further to see the stones or if they were lucky, to see them and to hear them falling as well. The little student was getting little sleep and losing much weight.

Mass Levi looked vexed and he had a right to be vexed. It was his property. How dare they throw stones on this man's roof? Or is know they don't know him? Everyone knew the full extent of Mass Levi's power. They knew it by fame or they knew it by fact. Those who hadn't known him in his early days, either because they weren't born yet or had not as yet arrived in Grove Town, had been told about him and could see for themselves how the power stood out in him. Mass Levi had been DC – district constable – in the old days and was not only physically strong and that obviously, but he was incorruptible. No one could blackmail him. No one could offer him a cut and get him to shut up. No woman could smile secretly when his name was called. He was a man who would use his cow cod whip on mule, on man and on woman though no one could say for certain that he ever had. And careful with God's time! You could set you clock by him.

Every Friday morning before day, you could hear Mass Levi urging his mules over Lee Bridge . . . "Come fair maid, come honey dripper" and as loving as their names were and as lovingly as he called their names, so he would lovingly put one little sting in their haunches in just the right spot with that cow cod whip which rumour said he kept soaked in their urine for better effect. Just one time he would give them that little sting. On Lee Bridge and they would go galloping into Tamarind Square. Then who was not ready to load their wares on the cart when Mass Levi reached the square would be left right there. He just didn't fool around.

He did not fool around with women either. Everybody knew that just as he appreciated good horse flesh, he appreciated a well-formed female body. But if any woman thought that God had given her that carriage to turn Mass Levi's head and give her any power over him, she could think again. Nevertheless he was very nice to them, and at the most unexpected times. For instance, he would come galloping his mules down to pick up the load with the sternest look on his face and say to Miss Madeline who was by then sitting beside him on the cart perspiring and wiping her face in her apron and praising the Lord that she had made it before Mass Levi drive off, "Miss Madeline, you are looking very admirable this morning". And he would stare silently at her until she lifted her eyes to him. Then he would smile promisingly and the smile would suddenly be replaced by benevolent pastoral chastisement "Control Miss Madeline, control". Clearly she was really at heart a loose woman who was sending signs of readiness to him. And the dear woman would be so ashamed, she would silently thank Mass Levi for saving her from sinning but in addition, for keeping her disgrace a secret. But she would never forget the possibilities which the moment had telegraphed. From then on, she would avert her eyes from him. But she knew that should nature call him, she would be very willing and ready. So while she averted her eyes, she would give a glance at him from time to time to see if he had a message. Many a matron sitting on those rugged Baptist benches was ready for Mass Levi. He had only to crook his pointer finger and she would come running and make all the arrangements to boot. But he never called.

He had his way with women, he had his way with the men. Same kind of way. You want two pounds to borrow and Mass Levi have it, it was never him to say no. "Here brother, freely you have received, freely give." Nor tell a single soul that things were hard with you. That was him. Could keep a secret. And not dunning you for it either. But he might see you with a glass of rum spree-ing your shirt and feeling fine, "Bertie, you a spree you shirt though" and with a little smile. Just that. And the rum would stop have taste. Many a man come to the Lord that way. Love Mass Levi and shame.

Is that said man why people yam stop get tief in Grove Town. Mass Levi catch the tief. You think him beat him? Mass Levi is a DC – Officer of the law. Him can carry him to the station, get him lock up, get him sentence and get him how much licks with the cat-o-nine and get him to spend how much years in prison. What him do? Mass Levi tie him like a hog on the patch fronting the square with one word: "Root. You like root up people field. You have your own now. Root."

Same thing with the ground. Whatever he plant grow. No magic. Not a single soul could a ever say they go to help Mass Levi fork him land and they find any good luck bottle buried anywhere. Hard work and coaxing. The man get up to catch the dew and didn't get home till lamplight. If a piece of ground refused to yield, is like he would say "Come darling why you treat me so?" Or some other nice word. "You want manure? Where you want it? Right here? No. Right here so then." Mass Levi know the very spot that lead under the ground from one point to the other and just the kind of nourishment his soil need and when, so he could put in just the right kind, in the right amount at just the right time to get the right result. You should see his bananas! Bunch big like ship and his callaloo, a sight to behold.

The man was blest and his fame travelled far and wide. Man with his owna privy! Thing only big massa have! Anywhere his children gave their names, people would say "the son of Levi Clarke?" and they would get good treatment.

33

He teach those children the merit of hard work and they were holding their own inside and outside of Grove Town. Just him and Miss Iris now and one young son left to fit out for life. You couldn't bet your money on children and though his had turned out well, Mass Levi never let anyone think that he thought his were by nature better than anyone else's. He tackled Calvert right there before everybody: "Son you have a hand in this?" and he pointed to the stones in his hands some of which Miss Euphemia had saved to show the curious. "She is a very nice and decent girl. You want her, ask. Nothing wrong. Come out and say it. Don't throw stones, spoil up the zinc and frighten the girl." As usual Mass Levi set the pace and others followed accusing their own boys and cautioning them. A fair man. A fair man is a powerful man. So which half-idiot boy could be joking round with the man and his property? Like them want to see the full extent of this man's power and want him to reel out his cow cod and get into action.

Only two people had any doubts about Mass Levi's powers. The one was Mass Levi himself and the other was his wife Miss Iris. She knew that now in his fifties, the poor dear man who had given her so much, watered her and made her grow, kept her protected from life's too hot sunshine and from the too much rain, was now but a shadow of himself. For all the pawpaw trees he was busy cutting down these days, he was still hanging like a dead rat. The stroke came on him suddenly and a man skilled at manipulation and given the gift of timing, a man who had conserved his energies for just the right moment was now weeping that his powers were gone. Fancy at that! Levi Clarke weeping. One whole year now. All that was left was memory. If prayers could help! If she knew where to find the power she would get it for him not so much for her sake as for his. Miss Iris watched him. Could he carry off this one?

Ole African saved him. The day he came down off the hill and walked around the house with his shut-pan, they knew. This was no human hand. This was no young man courting or young boys teasing. For Ole African only went where there was a spirit let loose needing to be cut and cleared. "The half has never been told," he muttered. And

34

Grove Town echoed it "The half has never been told, Ole African said." There was need for action. But not from Mass Levi.

SIX

A fit of singing came upon the Reverend Simpson. It was midday Friday and he had already done some visits. The spirit was preparing him for his Sunday sermon and it wanted to come in through song. It led him to "Let my people go". The Reverend had a fine baritone voice. "When Israel was in Egypt land/ Let my people go/ Oppressed so hard they could not stand/ Let my people go." And the meditation started. The words were coming quietly to the Reverend Musgrave Simpson. "That fellow in St. Ann. Fellow that start up this Aboukir Institute, is a good man. Hear he is trying to get the King to give him land in the Congo to begin some sort of return home. Fine. I endorse that. But that is not what 'go' means to me. That is 'go off' and it cannot be just 'go off' for they will follow you. What my 'go' means, is 'take your hands from off my shirt'." His voice was rising higher and higher. "What my 'go' means, is 'take your collar from my neck', is 'take your vyse from off my head', is 'stop sitting on my lungs and let me breathe'." The spirit was in flight now and it was taking his voice with it, higher and higher, clear through the ceiling. "'Let me go', 'let my spirit soar until it rises to the skies', 'let me see the burning bush'. He clothed Adam and Eve's disgrace, he will clothe ours too." Had it been Sunday and he was in the pulpit in the church, he would have clutched the rails till his knuckles stretched to membrane and his neck in its collar would have jerked repeatedly as he turned his mouth to the ceiling, and the vibrations in his voice would have started the V-shaped roof trembling. Then he would have simmered down to a whisper as he did now, "Lord give me the laws, the new covenant for this people."

It wasn't finished. He was still very warm and the blood was still pumping in starts through his body. He hummed. Then, "I have seen them take gold from the bowels of the earth to lock it in their museums. I have seen them take men's golden stools that God had taught them to carve and lock it in their museums. How much did Napoleon take? How much did Drake and Hawkins take? How do you measure men? In litres, pounds, in quarts? How much to sweeten how much tea? How much to make a garland for my lady's neck? Napoleon said to George: 'You see the stones in this necklace?' And George said to him, 'You see the jewels in my Crown?' People strung together in a chain." And the Reverend shook his head. "Separating people from themselves, separating man from his labour. Should be preparing to meet their God stead of stringing chains for aging queens. Spirit thieves!" The outburst tired him. "There is far too much anger in me" he said. "I have to deal with that before I can be ready." He was walking around the room and massaging his neck and shoulders to calm himself, to join the spirit back to flesh peaceably, but Maydene Brassington brought his ire to the fore again. "Off on her stout pretentious little walk to Grove Town again." He had rightly guessed her destination and there was some pretence in her business. He wondered what was going on.

There was pretence. Maydene told herself that she needed a bit of air and since she wanted to walk out a little bit, why not just walk down to Grove Town and since it was midday Friday, why not just go down into the village and take Ella up. It would be a bit early. And since it would be a bit early why not just stop by the Teacher's cottage and see if things were right with Amy Holness. In truth the news had reached Maydene Brassington's kitchen. Cook didn't get much of a chance to get out so Coachman had come and told her "Ole African said 'the half has never been told'. See here Cookie what a thing in this place eh!" If she had asked, she would have got an edited version. Maydene wanted to be on spot to feel and see the things with her own senses and that was why she was on her way to Grove Town. The spirit told Reverend Simpson to gird up his loins, put on his hat, jump on his steed, ride through the short cut and get there before her. His telephone was working well, for he was just about to get off the road and on to the short cut, when he saw the boy running towards him and waving. Mass Levi sent him with a message.

It said he thought a deacon's meeting as early as possible was necessary. He couldn't say much then, he said, only to say that strange things were happening which he thought called for a prayer meeting and a big one too. The bearer added one very important fact all on his own: Ole African was there.

As he and Betty picked their way up the hill, through the bush, down through the thick slippery mud, pushing away the high cutlass grass and the rose apple branches, Reverend Simpson remembered a time six hundred years ago.
I had tried. We did try. I had said to Willie.
- Willie, you are mightily fine, mighty fine. And it is true, was true, still is true. You sure can rattle those drums. You know it Perce.
- Darned if I don't - Perce had said.
- Perce, my Perce - I had said - Always had a soft spot for him. Soft, soft, spot. Always called him 'Perce'. Guess it was the very way he puckered his lips to play. Yeah 'pursed'.
- Perce - I had said. - You know that nobody can do what you do with a trumpet my man. And we know it too. Then there's me - I had said - Striking my own cymbals all the time, in time and that is good and we know it too. And I have a voice. We should play together.
He remembered a time five hundred years ago.
- Perce - I had said, - no one knows the stars better than you -
- Yeah, yeah, yeah - he had said - And Dan, no one picks up a scent better than you -
- Yeah, yeah, yeah, - I had said - And Willie is our main man with nose to the ground. Digging, always digging. Dig. No one knows the secrets of the earth better than he -
- Yeah, yeah, yeah - he had said.
He remembered a time four hundred years ago.
Yes. Willie shook me, woke me.
- Man, they are coming. Those nameless haunts. Dan - he had said.
- No one feels them vibes better than you. Tell it man -

38

– Perce, the time is now, – I had said – no one hits those
notes better than you. Crow man, crow, – I had said,
waking him.
– And who is our best secret eye – he had said – none but
our squealing Willie –
– We'll send them back to their tacky old ships – we had
said.
But they had come.
And just yesterday it seemed like – 1760 or was it 65? – we
had played it again.
I had said:
– Perce, no one knows the tree tops better than you. –
And Willie had said laughing:
– There is no better speleologist than I –
– Good word – I had said and we had all laughed and
they had said:
– Dan you have the teeth. We'll chase them from this
place to which they have brought us –
"Yeah, yeah", Parson Simpson sighed. "And here we are.
Some Spartans! Washed up on a rock drying our hair. Mistress
Maydene, this has got to change. So you take the low road and
I'll take the high road and I'll reach Grove Town afore ye. I have
got to this time." With the short cut and the horse, he beat her
to the centre of things. This time.

In the days before the stone throwing, Euphemia used to
put a long piece of lumber across the door and over two
wooden hasps nailed onto the wall beside the door. She
instructed the child to do likewise and she always did. That was
to protect them from intruders. But since the stone throwing,
that was out. She couldn't bother with that. Made no sense at
all. Those stones coulda open any door and come in. And what
is the sense of having them fly the heavy lumber off the hasps
and frighten the poor child once she fall off to sleep. Did not
make one ounce of sense! So now she just closed the door and
any little baby's hand could push it open.
Euphemia herself was deep into another world. That half-
sleep place where questions write themselves upon blackboards
before your very eyes. "Who I do anything bad? Tek wey few a
Puncie customers. But what is that? All in the business. If you

39

don't serve your customers good, dem no must go to somebody else? And that somebody just happen to be me. Puncie vex. Mi woulda vex too. But she really couldn't go a obeah man fi dat? No." And she giggled: "All now Woodcock mussi still a wait behind parish church. But nothing no eena dat fi anybody go obeah anybody bout. Just man and woman game." And she thought again: "Look how Wilberforce run wey before the baby born. And not a word. Mussi en tink mi coulden read. Den him moder come, come look see if a fi him." Now she sighed. Just a tiny one, still choked with the stale hurt that had brought Anita into the world. "A mi shoulda vex", she continued. "Now Taylor going have big wedding. Dress up beside Mary. Who going shame? No me. Den a why people a send spirit come stone my house?"

Euphemia had graduated to the thought that perhaps it wasn't really she but the girl that they were after and that she really should take her and go look, when the door flew open and she heard the child's scream. She, Euphemia had been lying beside her with her face fronting the door so is she should really have seen the thing first but her mind was far away. She only heard the voice say, "Yeah", when the child screamed and heard it say "The half has never been told". Is only afterwards the sight dawned on her and she saw that the greenish early dawn, the colour of young boiled breadfruit, was coming through the door which was now wide open and that a scarecrow was hanging from top to bottom in the doorway, its arms stretched out so that it seemed as if he were a rugged cross. And the stones started to come like never before. But none of them came into the house. They all landed on him. His blood was now sprinkling the steps. Then suddenly he left and the stones stopped. Euphemia would not have believed the thing had happened if she had not seen the natural blood upon the steps. Ole African had visited her in the flesh, so said those who knew or thought they knew. But apart from the blood the only physical sign of any mortal presence that Euphemia could show anybody, was the half-opened shut-pan in her kitchen which nobody said was theirs.

That is all Dan could see of his old friend Willie when he came. Some blood and some news of a shut-pan. Yes, he told

40

them, Ole African had been there and yes, the spirit had gone and yes, if he said "the half has never been told", it probably means that there are other things to come. And no, the shut-pan in the kitchen did not mean that the spirit had been driven into the kitchen. "Look at the blood," he said to them. "Look at what has been lost. The man is hungry and tired. Put some food in the shut-pan Euphemia. A straightforward matter." But Reverend Simpson knew it was no straightforward matter. He told Euphemia that the house was now safe, that her business was alright and that she could carry on as before. She had nothing to fear. "The little teenaged lady could do with a change", he added as if it were an afterthought, "I'll talk to Mrs. Holness."

SEVEN

If Selwyn Langley had been born in eighteenth or nineteenth century Britain and of upper class parentage, he would have been called a black sheep. He would have been sent off to Jamaica and would have met Ella O'Grady and chosen her from among his stock to be his housekeeper. He would have given her two children, made his fortune and returned to England as an ordinary sheep ready for his rightful place in the fold there and she would have been left with a small consideration, and her children, with what she could make of it, along with their very profitable skin colour. But this chap was American and not even upper class. He was from a long line – long for America – of chemists, manufacturers of herbal medicines and today doctors and travelling medical lecturers. And this was on both sides of the family so there was quite a little empire being built up for Selwyn to inherit. The thing was that he had no interest whatsoever in boiling or measuring herbs or in sounding chests, and though he was a charming fellow and could sell just about anything, herbal medicine was not one of the things he intended to sell. The "What are we going to do with him?" which inevitably came after the family gathering had cracked its collective sides listening to his jokes, was a real question which Elsinore and Daisy preferred to phrase "What are we going to do?" since he was their heir and since Elsinore it was, who had pulled together medicine-making, doctoring and the publishing of medical literature into a building called the Langley Complex from which the Langley healing technique and the Langley cures radiated all over the world. It was hard to have to see some brother's child as emperor.

Selwyn was the world's biggest practical joker. He was also kind. He didn't stick around to smart his parents' eyes. He went off of his own accord with a group of Baltimore-based players. Motion pictures were being talked about and Selwyn talked vaguely about them, so that those who wanted to glorify themselves through their blood could tell themselves and others that the Langley heir was going to extend the family interests into that new line of business. "My dear, he is ever so funny! His time is coming." Until it came, Selwyn occupied himself with one production: the making of Ella O'Grady. Ella had come over with Mrs. Burns. In the same preoccupied way that she had trotted around behind Mrs. Brassington, totally unaware that there were places the parson's English wife could sit that she couldn't, Ella had trotted pass the immigration clerk behind Mrs. Burns with nary a glance and come into the United States of America as white. It was Selwyn who explained to her in simple terms that she was coloured, mulatto and what that meant, taking her innocence with her hymen in return for guidance through the confusing fair that was America. Ella was hooked and she liked the drug.

There was the powdering and the plucking of eyebrows, the straightening of the hair, all of which a loving husband did and just in case, just in case there should he the rare occasion on which she would be called upon to wear a no-sleeved bathing dress, he taught her the habit of shaving her armpits. And it was fun for they shaved together. The creator loved his creature. He mightn't, Selwyn thought to himself, be able to make prophylactics, but he could make a story live. Ella played well. She had a lifetime of practice and her little just-me-come methodist soul told her there was no harm in it. Just one teeny little lie: her parents had come from Ireland, had succumbed to a tropical disease and she had been left by them to be brought up by a methodist parson and his wife. The truth could hardly make an appearance and embarrass anyone. Mrs. Burns knew very little more about her than that she had been the ward of the Brassingtons who indeed were a methodist parson and his wife. And in her whole year of marriage, Ella had never been called upon to tell this tale. In fact, in all of America, no one but Selwyn seemed interested in her and her past. He loved her life story and there she was because of it, the happiest little married lady on earth. And if he wanted her to be full Irish girl, well what of it? There was just one little thing that she couldn't brush off. No big thing yet . . . after a whole year, there was no little Ella forthcoming. This was beginning to disturb her, but just.

* * * * * *

– May, you have become quite a village wench. Must be these visits to Grove Town. – And the Reverend William Brassington slapped his wife Maydene on her behind. In mock surprise she shrieked:
– William, you have become quite a lad yourself. Must be those visits to Grove Town. Somebody's been teaching you things – and she turned him around by his ear.
– Who is she? –
– Miss Gatha – he replied. And they collapsed laughing like they were twenty years younger than they were.

The Reverend William Brassington had just finished making love to his wife Maydene and for the second consecutive weekday. Ever since she had connected herself to those people, there had been these changes. Even in those heady first days of marriage, they had restricted themselves to Sunday nights. He had finished the hardest day of God's work and he needed the break and renewal. But in the past three years things had changed. At first, it was just Wednesday nights that had crept in to join Sunday, but now he had noticed that Thursday was beginning to enter the fray as well. Not that he minded.

– William, love, there is a problem – Maydene spoke. She was bent over the washstand with her back to him, her voice muffled by the towel with which she was drying her face. William froze in the middle of his dressing, bent his knees slowly and sat on the bed, and let his braces drop. He was waiting for the concrete. – Yes May, I know. These days I feel everything that bothers you. – And the muscles in his face did twitch. – Your ministry is so heavy. – The sarcasm had long gone out of such comments. He had by now come to accept that hers was ministerial work as well.

– It is our business this time, William. Very close to home. I know it. – His twitch got worse. He was picking up the enormity of the problem and without her having to tell him, he knew that it was the worst. Not the boys. He could handle

44

that. It was Ella. Whatever happened to her was his fault. He
it was who had engineered her migration from the family,
from Grove Town, from Morant Bay and from Jamaica, and
into Baltimore, USA.
– Ella – he said. And she nodded. Maydene stared through the
frosted bedroom window as if she could see some writing
beyond:
– It has just begun, but it is going to be bad, very bad – she
said. Sensing her husband's shudder, she added:
– There is nothing we can do about it. It will pass – It had
always happened for William that fear went when the
revelation came. So it did now. The twitch and the shudder
went and he saw his function clearly. It was to be where he
could help when he was needed.
– I will be here – he said, thinking that he really had no
choice. It was he who had sent her into that strange setting.
And in any case where else could he be? This was home.
Wasn't it?

* * * * * *

No shiny green banana trees here flat-footed in the
ground, brown-trunked windmills and erect. No blue lagoon.
No raindrops, fat and thick beating through the tin roof. No
black people. Here were fine pines with leaves so dainty she
could not separate them from the green globe that their heads
made. And here was the perpetual cloud sometimes like
young smoke, sometimes like an early morning Grove Town
fog. It was all quite familiar. They hadn't shown her that in
school, but she had learnt of Britain and of Norway and had
been all about the temperate zone with her story-book friends.
Baltimore was nothing new.
Mrs. Johnny Burns was the sister of the manager of the
one hotel on Jamaica's north coast. Naturally, she lived
wherever she chose to live, on the right side of the tracks, and
naturally the people in her world looked like her. So here
where she lived in Baltimore there were no Reverend
Simpsons, black and with a mouth stretching from one side of
his face to the other like a bulldog and looking just as stern;
no Ole African with his dreadful hair; no Mass Levi with black

45

palms, finger nails, gums and not even Mammy Mary with skin dark cream like the sweet potato. Here there were only adult Peter Pans, Dairy Maids and Lucy Grays and a fair sampling of their relatives seen not in daily intercourse but now and again when they floated in through the big oak door, with their umbrellas and overcoats, on appointment. This was the kind of life – pale-skinned people floating – that Ella had seen for most of the many years of her daydreaming existence.

This trip to Baltimore was the first time Ella was travelling with her body. The winter might have shocked that body and the mind it housed, into perceiving the difference between fantasy and reality, into the fact that it was born and acclimatized to 80°F and was now being asked to survive in 30°F and below, but the Johnny Burns were rich, rich, rich and had a thing called central heating. Ella was Mrs. Burns sidekick, her little dolly baby and she dressed her in warm finery. So it was only on the odd occasion that she got a fleeting sensation of something lost – the yellow fire of the sun in St. Thomas, Jamaica.

Ella in a range of animal skins went to this social and that, this lecture and that, quietly waiting on Mrs. Burns. A silent Alice waiting on the Duchess. Very quiet. A marvellously sculpted work waiting for the animator. That was what Selwyn Langley saw. It was with this vision before him that he fully realized that movie-making was indeed going to be his line. He looked at Ella long and smiled: here was the future, after all that hide and seek! Ella saw someone like Peter Pan smiling at her and knew that she was feeling particularly warm. The Baltimore temperature raised itself several degrees up for them. Ella was hot to melting.

When the green pines turned to grey and the snow began to fall, Selwyn learnt that he wanted to see Ella's eyes open at the delight of feeling the snowflakes on her body; that he wanted to watch her watch these falling flakes through his glass window; that he wanted to be in that room alone with her, to light a fire and have her take him into a tropical December and have her show him its jungle and tell him its strange tales. Selwyn could get a nut to let itself out of a shell, but he could not get Mrs. Burns to budge. No. He could not teach her ward drama. He could not get that hag to give up half an hour of her doll. So Selwyn saw to it that he was where Mrs. Burns was, that he opened her doors, that he pulled out her chairs, that he was the soul of wit. But no. He could not get Ella to go to the 300 with him. Mrs. Burns was beginning to enjoy the chase. He could come in. But no. He could not see Ella alone. Yet his whole career now depended on animating that doll. What about marriage? She could not sanction that. Ella has a father. See him. Then the nut took action. Ella engineered her escape for a few hours to his room.

Ella had yet to be kissed, but the noble young man took her back to Mrs. Burns, explained where they had been and shyly declared that he was as always willing to marry. She in turn let the couple know that she was very upset: they had disgraced her. What could she tell the Reverend Brassington? A wedding breakfast was all they could get. Mrs. Burns was enjoying the drama. Better than all the plays she had been dragging herself to and here she was both actor and director. The young man was witty, seemed to care for the girl and was decent, and after all, the girl had to marry sometime and a travelling player was usually broadminded. She had done well. Ella was getting on – nearly eighteen now. What better was there for her? That's what Mrs. Burns wrote to tell the Reverend Brassington. She knew no more of the fellow's background, she told him, than what the young man had told her: his father was a chemist somewhere in the mid-west but he did not want to follow that line and had come east to make something of himself in a form that he saw fitting to his talents. Mrs. Burns promised that she would keep an eye on the couple on the Reverend Brassington's behalf. Ella's growing pains began.

EIGHT

Five years ago when Maydene Brassington first went to visit Amy Holness, Mary Riley had got their message and had gone to the teacher's cottage. She had later gone on to Morant Bay to the methodist manse and had come home to think over what the ladies had said. No. She didn't mind at all. Didn't mind sharing Ella. For that was what the lady said. Parson's wife. Parson Brassington that is. The lady said that a child should have two parents. Two people should share the load and since the child didn't have a father, she and Parson would act as father, something like godparents. She said that she Mary had carried the load by herself for all these years and could do with a little break. So after a few years when her age was up in school, she and Parson would take on the burden completely and see to it that she was fitted out for life. But right now, it was sharing. Ella would stay with Mary and continue to go to Grove Town School but on Friday evenings she would come to the mission house in Morant Bay and stay there until Sunday evening. Not to worry about clothes. She would see to the clothes that Ella would wear while she was in her house. That sounded real fine.

No. Mary didn't mind at all. Because what? To tell the truth, she was becoming a bit worried. The worry began when Ella started to see her health. Anything could happen to her and with she Mary down the wharf on weekends and up at property sometimes during the week there was nobody to protect the child. The district children still called her all sorts of names. She knew that that meant that they were curious about Ella. It worried her that some little boy's curiosity would one day get the better of him and the next thing she would know is that Ella would come home with her clothes torn off her back and something in her belly. It was worse now that she was springing breasts and soon needing something to hold them up. And slim little Ella was spreading at the hips. Must be the father's blood for her people were

48

slim, slim, slim. Taylor had teased her and said "All them who was laughing, soon want touch, for seeing is believing but touching is the naked truth" and he would sing the last part. Taylor was like that, so jokify. But it was a true word. True word.

Then there was Taylor. Long time now he been around. Running around. Four, five children now and not living with any of the baby mother them. Telling her that it is her fault. That he want to settle down and make a decent man of himself. Well pass him 30 now, a year from 40. Want to set up the blacksmith business on a good footing, want to join a church and go out Sunday mornings like a big man, want to pull all his children together. "You see Mass Levi, that is a big man. Everything under one cover. Nobody calling his name on anything. No need hide from anybody. They want you, they come to you. So man to stay! And is because him have Miss Iris to pull things together with him. One finger can't kill nit." She was the woman to help him pull his life together. He had always told her so. If she had been with him long time, he wouldn't have been having them patchwork children – one here, one all over the place. Thirteen years now.

From the time she had come back from Morant Bay with the belly, and he noticed that no one was coming around to claim it, he had made his way to her door and in a very proper manner offered to take it. That time he must have been about twenty-five. Came in his full drill suit with his shirt buttoned right up to his neck. And shoes. Dressed like Sunday on the Friday evening. Didn't bother with any story about just passing by. Had come right to the point. He had been watching her for a long time. From she was young girl in school. And just when he thought he could put that kind of question to her, she had gone off to Morant Bay. It wasn't too late. He had still been watching and he didn't see anyone coming around, so would she let him act the part. She had cried and he had held her.

Taylor was a couple years older than her well. Must have been in 'bout sixth book about to leave school when she was in third book, or even lower down. Remembered her first and only fight – a nearly fight really. The bigger ones had wanted a display and they were pushing her and another little one – can't even remember who now – on to each other hoping that one would push the other away and a fight would begin. The other one was warming up, ready to go into action when Taylor from his huge height, or so it seemed then, came up with "Leave the little pickney them alone," and she was saved. And whenever storms threatened she would glance around and know that he was there. But she didn't know that he thought of her in that way. He was popular, always in demand, he could play the fiddle and the fife and they had put his name with Delaceita who was dancing own master. He had come. And had put a very sensible argument to her. "You one can't manage. No see Miss Kate can't help herself?" She had cried and cried, but she had shaken her head. No. And she had told him: she wasn't going to let him carry a whiteman's child. He would be a laughing-stock. Let her carry her own disgrace. That way it would pass off quicker. She was adamant.

He had continued to come around. Sometimes he carried a little parcel of liver if it was a Friday evening: "Quick, cook this for me May" – he used to call her May though he knew full well she was Mary. Said he was christening her himself. Sometimes it was a couple fingers of plantain and Mary didn't bother to try to resist because she knew that Taylor knew that things were short with her and he had come to help her and she was not going to insult a kindness which she needed by refusing it. When she decided to build the little house in her mother's yard, Taylor was right there helping her to organize. Seemed he always let anyone who was his woman at the time know that they couldn't come between him and her because no one ever tried to fight her and she knew Taylor had plenty women. Many more times he would suggest that he move in with her and they become man and woman. Her answer was always. "No. Taylor you don't want to tie up yourself with a strange woman and her strange daughter." He had always laughed it off, gone off to some woman and would always come back, sometimes complaining about the woman, sometimes laughing at how he had had to part two of them and that kind of thing.

This last time he had come differently though. Like the

50

first time he had come this time, hat in his hand and standing. He had called her Miss Mary Riley and said this was Newton James addressing you. "As you know my father is a tailor (that's why they call me Taylor). Not living with my mother like your father and mother, but my grandmother bring me up respectable and my father had enough to school me and send me to trade. I am a saddler and a blacksmith by trade and I can more than support myself and you and whoever you carry. I am asking you to let me be the man." That first time, her mother had been in the room next door them and could hear everything; he had been with her in the hall. "Miss Kate knows everything already, so I am not hiding. But is you I have to talk to before I go back and make my request of her." And she had turned him down. He had made a monkey face and they had laughed and left it there. He had come back this time in the same way: "My father was . . . I am . . . I am asking you to let me be the man . . . " He was very very serious this time. He added that he had been seeing Euphemia. Yes, she knew that. She was giddy but she was settling down. He hadn't asked her any proper question but he was ready to settle down and if it wasn't she Mary, he was going to try Euphemia. Marriage before a parson was going to be in it this time and if it wasn't she, there wasn't going to be much visiting between because he didn't want her pulling him this way and Euphemia the other. He was now going to pull in a team. It was for her to decide if she was going to be in the team. He was very serious this time. No laughing. No monkey face. He had left and said that he would come back end of month. It was now mid month.

So it was deliverance when the lady asked about Ella. She couldn't give Ella what she needed. She had faced that. Ask Ella to scald the little milk and you would hear the phew-phew and smell the milk going down the side of the pot and being burnt by the flames. Ella was right there in the kitchen but she had made the milk boil over! Nothing left in the pot. Or simply ask her to roast two cocoes. By the time you call Ella to bring them to the table, you would get nothing but a loud silence because Ella fraid to tell you she can't find the cocoes. Can't find? The cocoes turn bright red fire. Is true what people did tell her. Ella was not bush mout pickney. So the lady was going to fit her for life. That good. And she would have Ella with her for two more years every weekday. In any case whatever path God had chosen for her, it would not be long before all kinds of calls of nature would separate them from each other and she would be left without a soul to call her own. And according to Taylor she would lose him too.

Marriage have teeth and she wasn't too much for those certain things but she could work hard. Perhaps they could make it. They would have to draw on something more upon the house. Was only a room and hall. Ella could get the room for now until she go up to mission house. They would have to draw on a room for the two of them. It would have to be her house. She wasn't leaving go nowhere. Moreover, Taylor's shop was too near the road with everybody stopping by. Too difficult for people to understand that things change. Let him keep the shop out there and then at night-time he come home. Yes. That seemed alright. And as a matter of fact, with Ella going up in the world, it would suit her to have a married mother so everything would turn out alright. It was just that she didn't know Taylor in those ways. There had only been the man O'Grady and she never so much did like it to all that. Guess them things never mek to like. She had to try it though. When Taylor come next time, she would tell him that she would give it a try. Lord. Wedding is expense, and all them people looking at you. Wonder if Taylor would let them go quietly to Town and come back. No. And she laughed to herself. "Mi know Taylor. Him going want to fling him foot and mek speech." That is one more thing to get accustomed to. But it wouldn't be now. House have to extend and all that. Money have to find for it, so she really had plenty time to get used to the idea and to talk out more things with Taylor. He had said he "wanted everything under one cover". She wondered whether he was expecting her to be mother to all his children. That she must ask. That would call for bigger house and more beds to be built and all kind of things. This thing might really have teeth fi true!

But it would work. Then she worried a little bit about Ella, whether she was doing the right thing by her. "Taylor say the man no too righted. 'Parson read too much book,' him say, 'That's why him can't look straight in people eye. Is just that.

But the woman have sense.' Is him Taylor look after them buggy. So that is another thing. Though him live right here, he know 'bout what go on in the mission house. And him and Mr. Smith that drives for them is his bosom friend, so he will keep an eye on Ella. And nothing fi hinder me from go dey go haul wey mi pickney if she nah meet no good treatment." What a lot of change! She could hardly wait the two weeks for Taylor to come. "Guess as him hear that Parson wife was looking for me, he will come to see why." But Mary changed her mind and decided not to wait. She would begin the revolution. After all if she was going to make her life with Taylor, she might as well begin to meet him half-way and so she betook herself down to his shop to tell him how things were. And he said it made sense, so Maydene Brassington began coming down to Grove Town on Fridays to take Ella O'Grady home with her to the house in Morant Bay for the weekends.

NINE

– It was really the Anita business why Parson decide to take me and send me to train at Port Antonio. Then Mrs. Shard see me and love me and ask Parson to let me stay in her house and get the training there while keeping the company of the children and going to school. Then she and the children leaving going back home to England and I finish with school and they figure I train enough and she and Parson speak to Mrs. Burns and she say, Yes, she could do with a companion, so that is how I come here. –

When she was telling her stories of back home. Ella always fell into broken English. It excited Selwyn. She told him of the poltergeist:

– Yes, I see the stones with my own eye. – And his eyes popped. – Yes, yes, see them falling. Hear them and pick up some too. Small gravel. Some people say they even see rock stone fall on haunted house, but only gravel fall on this one. – She told him about the blood on the steps and his eyes popped wider.

– You really saw it? –

– Really see it: I didn't see Ole African though. But people say that he stop at the front door of the house with his hands stretched out like he was a cross. – And she had to pull every little bit of information that she had anywhere in her head on Ole African, out for him. Poltergeists he had heard about but a little village full of black people and one living in the hills and twice as wise as they were old, had never before dawned on Selwyn's consciousness. Ella told him of her own brush with Ole African.

It was a Friday evening shortly after Mrs. Brassington had taken to going down into the village to collect Ella to take her to the manse for the weekend. It was in that same week that the poltergeist stopped and that Anita moved up to the teacher's cottage. What happened was that Mrs. Brassington

54

had gone around to see Mrs. Amy Holness and had stayed too late. It was later than her usual late when she and Ella were hurrying across the pasture near to the cane-piece and when they saw the scarecrow high in the air walking as if on two roots of sugar cane.

"My God, this is really possible?" Mrs. Brassington said aloud. She had heard of Africa's stiltmen and Ole African had been all about her ears recently. Here he was before her very eyes.

Ole African's clothes were old and torn and so dirty, the bits fell like strips of leather around his waist. His hair was the same story but here the strips of leather were thinner though about the same length as those around his waist and which hung to his knees.

– Do you know him child? – Mrs. Brassington had asked Ella. No child in Grove Town needed to see Ole African to know him. They had been hearing about him for centuries. He was the arch punisher. Mrs. Brassington might not have known that and might truly have meant to ask Ella, "Have you seen him before?", but Ella knew the right question and the right answer and deliberately chose to respond to Mrs. Brassington literally: – No, I do not know him. –

Cold bumps gathered on her flesh as she retold the story. That happening had then, and the memory of it did now, send a sharp electric shock through her body. It was her answer – "No, I do not know him" – which shocked her then and now, but Ella had not as yet reached this truth and Selwyn couldn't help her. He saw her shudder and saw behind that the horrible sight of Ole African. What delightful theatre!

Ella told him about Mrs. Brassington, how the sight of the tattered old man swinging through the air drove her to her knees in prayer right there in the night on the ground in the pasture. She was so frightened, she told him.

– She said "Leave" and she take my hand and we walk home as fast as our feet could carry us. – And that was another part of the story that caused Ella some worry as she retold it. If Mrs. Brassington was talking to her, she would have said "Let us leave" but she didn't. She had said "Leave". Just once. She could have been talking to Ole African. But in that case, she would have shouted to him "Leave". But she didn't shout.

She said it very softly. Her story seemed to her now to have some part missing but she dismissed the thought and pressed on to give Selwyn her version of how the Anita story came to make the Reverend Brassington decide to take matters into his hands and send her off to Port Antonio.

On that night of which Ella had been speaking, Mrs. Brassington had checked the time and then said to her Lord quietly:

"Equip us dear Lord with the armoury for spiritual warfare and teach us how to pray". Communication seemed to move into action as she screwed her face, clenched her fists and pulled all the power she could find from inside of her and anywhere else with which she was in touch. With all her energies spent in pulling her forces together and in focusing them elsewhere, all that she could manage to give voice to was "Leave". And with that she got up from her knees, took Ella's hand and tried to make for home as fast as she could to allay William's usual fears of her walking in the bushes at night alone and to share with him this other-worldly experience.

As Ella saw it, the turmoil in Grove Town had not ended with the cessation of the stone-throwing, and that was most certainly true. The half had indeed not been told.

– It was Parson who this time talk to Mammy Mary and ask if I could stay full time at the manse. With all this wandering spirit and this evil around, and nobody knowing when the stones would start again or where, Parson say that I should not be down there, having to come up after dark with Mrs. Brassington. I think too that she must be tell him about Ole African in the cane-piece. Whatever . . . I start living full time at the manse. He didn't even want me to go back there to school and then he hear about this high school in Port Antonio that would train me and they had to send me down in the buggy every day. Then Mrs. Shard speak to Parson and I stay with her and then go back to the manse on weekends and then I start staying with her all through the term and going home for holidays and then I start staying with her even for some holidays and then I finish my training and you know the rest. –

Ella had not told the half. She did not know it. She did not

56

know for instance that the spirit had followed Anita right up to the teacher's cottage. That house had two bedrooms. Since the Holness' had no children or any other people living with them, they had turned the spare bedroom into a study for Teacher. It held his books and his organ. Under normal circumstances, this would have been the ideal place for Anita: she could read until her eyes were sore and she could hear the notes of the organ rather than having to figure them out in her head. Right now though her first need. was sleep and in any case, Reverend Simpson had strongly suggested that she should keep away from any occupation which forced her into solitary mind expansion. So there was to be no truck with the books and the organ. That the child shouldn't be inside of herself but with company, suited Mrs. Holness: she could enjoy the presence of another female helping her in the kitchen, sewing with her, washing and plaiting their hair together and doing all the little female things which she thought mothers and daughters did.

Anita was alright in the days. There were a lot of little women's tasks that she knew she could learn from Mrs. Holness and which she wanted to learn and which her own mother couldn't teach her, either because she didn't know how to do them or didn't have the facilities or didn't have the time. Take baking for instance. Miss Phee, as Anita's mother Euphemia was called for short, just didn't have the time to grate potatoes, grate coconuts, find and grate nutmegs and mix them up to make a potato pudding. Potatoes she had; coconuts she had too and the house kept sugar of course and all the other condiments needed. There were no currants there but Miss Amy said that they weren't necessary. There was a dutchie pot in which the pudding could have been baked. There was no stove and there was no coal at home to make the baking easy but there again Miss Amy said it didn't matter much what kind of fire you used while you managed to have hell at top and hell at the bottom and the hallelujah in the middle – and they had laughed at the way she had put it. Wood was good enough she said, or even coconut husks. What was important she said was that you regulate the fire to suit the stages of the cooking. That

Euphemia had no time for, so there was no baking in her house. Only boiling. Then there was crocheting and things like drawn thread-work and framing pictures in passe-partout which she Anita wanted to do and she could look forward to doing in Miss Amy's company. The days were alright and looked as if they were going to be alright.

It was the nights which gave everyone trouble. Every night but not all through the night. For that they were thankful. Just the mornings and the evenings at about 8 p.m. On the first night Teacher and Miss Amy heard sobbing and a muttering sound like pleading coming from Anita's room. It stopped quickly and they dismissed it as the normal symptoms of a tired mind. It happened again in the morning at about five. Same kind of sounds. They didn't worry too much. Nightmares they could handle. Much better than they could stone-throwing and they were glad that that hadn't followed her. It was when the sound remained regular, coming at 8 p.m. every night and 5 a.m. every morning and becoming so loud that they could hear Anita's word clearly: "I don't want you to touch me please" that they became a little worried. But there was a solution. Having company in bed as well as at the day's chores might help. And since the spare room was so small, made smaller by the organ and the books, Teacher moved over there and let Anita share his bed with Miss Amy.

But Anita's disturbance didn't stop. And it wasn't no nightmare either, not unless you are willing to believe that a nightmare is catching. When Miss Amy began to feel things too, the Holness' decided that there was more than they could handle without guidance and called upon Reverend Simpson. Anita's pleadings had continued right on time every day for the two weeks before the Holness' sought help. On their first night together, Miss Amy, wanting to calm and protect the child, had stretched out her hand to hug her and thought she felt a body between them. She kept the thought to herself: her imagination was playing tricks. Must have imagined that Jacob was there between them on the bed. But the sense of the third body continued. Then one morning it boxed away her hand as she stretched it out to the child and on another morning pinned her hands down on her side so

58

that she was moaning in discomfort and fright. She couldn't bring herself to talk about any of this. If she left it where it was in her head, she argued, it couldn't get to her. To Anita's cries of "please don't touch me" were now added, twice daily at 8 p.m. and at 5 a.m., Miss Amy's moanings as whoever or whatever it was tried to pin her hands to her side to keep her from comforting Anita. Reality had now become distorted for Amy Holness and she was frightened. So it was with great relief that she shared her experiences with her husband when he asked:
– Amy, something is going on. What is it? –

Reverend Simpson listened to the stories told by the three of them, then he sent Anita to the kitchen to help his housekeeper to prepare and serve the lemonade and then said:
– Mrs. Holness, you might have heard older mothers, even your own mother say of her children "I fight with them to bring them where they are". When in the future you talk of all this – if of course Anita stays with you – you will have to say "I fought for her". Do you want to say that? This child is in trouble. It could be dangerous for you too. – For Jacob's sake she would have said "Yes" and taken on the job whatever the dangers. But it wasn't just Jacob nor even the preservation of Anita though that was now important to her. Miss Amy remembered her dream. It was the dream. She didn't know how, but she had a strong feeling that what was happening was connected to it. It came to her that this was her chance to swim across that water. She didn't know why she had to, but every part of herself told her that this was her gethsemane and it didn't suit her to put it off.
But how to fight? She looked at Reverend Simpson. Clearly he had said all that he had to say on the matter. The visit had ended. There was just the mandatory social part to get over with, the lemonade to be served and drunk, a few "oh's" to be exclaimed and some "ha ha's" to be laughed and a little bit of gossip to be got through:
– Teacher, Mrs. Brassington has taken a shine to you. Ha ha. –
– She smells blood Parson and it is not mine. Ha ha. –
– Oh? Then whose? –
– Ella. –

– Ella? Who? Oh, the little one who recited? Now isn't that just fair. "Take up the whiteman's burden . . ." Ha ha. Remember that Teacher. So you brought them together! Ha ha. – Then the never-ending lines of "how is . . ." How is Mass Levi doing? How are his children doing? Whatever became of . . .

TEN

Miss Iris did not know whether to be glad or sorry that Calvert was still living at home. She was glad for she needed the little company, somebody to share thoughts with. She was sorry, for the boy and his father were always rowing and creating confusion in her life for she didn't know which side to take. Truly, the father seemed to be picking on the child. How could she take the child's side openly? You couldn't do that. How could she in the quiet of the bedroom where man and wife should trash out differences, counsel the father, when the man was turning his stiff back to her night after night till she felt so afraid of touching him that instead of jumping over him to use the chamber pot like she had done for years, she now found herself shuffling down to the foot of the bed and jumping over that onto the floor and pulling the vessel to one side of the room rather than use it in front of him like she used to. The thing was turning her heart to cold stone. Levi was gone away from her. Ever since the night when he had cried, he had moved out of reach. There are several ways of going to church. Everybody knew that and she had told Levi so. She was a big old woman. Calvert, her baby was seventeen and she had started on to grandchildren. What she going want children now for, even if her womb had not dried up yet. Whatever he did or could do, was the same husband. And didn't she take him for better or for worse? "No half measures", he said. And that was that.

Levi was a strong man. And spiritually too. He always said that every problem has a solution. And lived by that. There were problems before. Some he would tell her about, some he wouldn't talk about but whose existence she would guess. He had a leave-it-to-me attitude and it had worked before. All that she could ever do was to get down on her knees and pray that he be strengthened to go through. In what would seem like no time, one night after the bedroom door was shut, he would put on a voice gruffer than his usual to frighten her and would say "I want to speak to you". And she would wonder about what and it would come out in a smile that he couldn't hide: "You remember such and such (sometimes this was the first time she was hearing the problem named), well, is alright now." In the early days she had asked how. But he never answered. Just wanted the congratulations and she was never tardy about giving that because she loved him and she was proud of him. But this thing was different. This problem and the solution could not be hidden from her not as long as they shared the same bed. And since they had no mansion, they would be in the same bed with the problem for God knows how long.

Since Levi, her husband, had taken himself away from her, it was natural that Miss Iris would get closer to her young son. Her problem apart, the boy was her wash-belly and special, and he was now moving into manhood with all its strange feelings and she had to make sure that there was a heart and a soul ready to make sense of it for him for Levi was just nowhere, off-key. Take for instance the girl and the stones. Miss Iris was shocked into whispered words at the father's bad reading: "The man go ask him if him have anything fi do with that and before crowd too. But what wrong with Levi after all? How him can't see say the little boy heart a break over the little child? Go ask him that!" Her son needed her. And she needed him and that was another reason why she was partly sorry that he was still around. A child so sensitive, was guessing that something was bothering her and was trying to protect her and that was only bringing down Levi's ire upon his head. "Calvert go throw stone frighten anybody! The man don't know this child anymore? Levi gone. What to do?" She answered herself: "Nothing to do but pray".

A lot of praying was going on in that house. Mass Levi was praying extra hard too. They still had their morning prayers and their Sunday service together all three of them. But about three weeks now, Mass Levi had been getting up early in the mornings and taking his Bible and his books into the privy with him and spending a good hour there. Same thing at nights. "But if he read so much with that tinen lamp when the problem over he bound to be blind" Miss Iris was thinking. "Thank God for Jesus though" she continued in her wry meditation, "it is those hours with his God that make him able to still walk powerful as if nothing is wrong." Then Mass Levi added something new which really hurt his wife. He was now fasting. "What am I for?" she said to herself. "Not even cooking for my husband? Mercy!"

* * * * * *

Everybody thought that Teacher and his wife should go and look about Anita. Euphemia thought so too and thought that since she hadn't heard that they had, perhaps she should go and take her child and go look, but she figured that she couldn't just go up there to the cottage and take her since the Reverend Simpson and everybody had said that was the best place for her. She had no big bag of money but she had her business; this was her only child and many a person would lend her what they had to see her through this, especially as they were all looking at her and asking her what she was going to do about the one pickney she birth, if she going to stand by while Teacher and Miss Amy did nothing. Nobody had heard anything new had happened but wasn't it just common sense to see that the thing had been after the child? What Miss Phee had to lose? It was the child who had brains and was bright and was looking like she was going to go far. Bad-minded people wanted to take away the child's spirit. And didn't Ole African say "The half has never been told". That meant that it could happen again. The least Euphemia or whosoever was in charge of the child should do is get her a guard. Euphemia thought it through carefully and considered that she would wait until something else happened and make a case to Miss Amy to give her back the child so that she could go look some protection. Had she known why the three had gone to visit Reverend Simpson, she would surely have made her move. As it was, Anita kept the business right there in the house and was looking so loved that Euphemia could not get a clue.

Miss Amy herself wondered whether she should go and try to see. There were lots of things that would make her hesitate. The main one was money. She wasn't totally sure that the lack of any firm advice from Reverend Simpson did not really mean that he thought she should go and find somebody who knew. But the money. She had none and where was Teacher to get it from when they couldn't even find money to give her own a start with a sewing machine? And the risk to Teacher's reputation of the manager or the inspector knowing that his wife was in contact with an obeah man. Even if that could be arranged, if she could go to a far place where nobody knew her, where was the money to come from? All that thinking was brought to an abrupt halt.

Somehow or other, Maydene Brassington learnt what people were saying was meant by Ole African's "the half has never been told" and like the thinking woman she was, she expected trouble for those at the teacher's cottage. She didn't know that anything had started happening as yet but had overheard talk in her kitchen about the need for an obeah man. Over she flew to counsel Mrs. Holness. Now, even if Miss Amy could find the money and could find a person far enough away so that she would not endanger her husband's career, how could she keep the truth of a cure – and a cure was the point of going to see – from this inquisitive woman who had grafted herself on to her family?

– Somebody is fooling you people that only you know about the occult. The things I have heard and seen in my own country would as you say here, Mrs. Holness, make your head grow. No. It is tempting but don't go to the conjuror. You would be giving somebody else control over your spirit and good as he might be, that could be dangerous, it is unhealthy. –

Miss Amy looked at the pink-faced lady and was annoyed. "These people", she was thinking, "always think they know more about your business than you do and besides always think that they have a right to tell you so." Much as she would like to shut her out, tell her her pot was boiling over and have her leave, she couldn't, for this was no ordinary busybody neighbour, this was the Reverend's wife, the wife of the man in charge of so many schools; this was high class, the Reverend's English wife. There was nothing else to do but to hope that the lady would vanish of her own accord and leave her to her business. Then Mrs. Brassington did something which swept her off her feet. She raised her chin, lowered her eyelids, looked her up and down from the corner of her eye, stared at her for a few seconds and snorted – "Hmm". There was no better native put down. "You are a child. How would you know? Why should I bother to present my credentials to you?" it said. "This lady is more than meets the eye", Miss Amy thought in shock and then relaxed a bit. Then Mrs. Brassington face softened and she said: – But I am not being fair to you. You couldn't know. Some clergymen in the Christian church are taught how to handle spirits. My father was one, – and she continued more gently – Don't reject my offer. I'll help you to pray while you fight. Now I must go and collect Ella. It is already dark. – And with that she raised her massive frame from the little bentwood chair and strode into the night. A couple feet from the steps, she stopped, turned around and threw a whisper to Miss Amy, who now more confused than ever, was waiting for her to leave so she could find some way of making sense of what had just happened.

– I have only watched and read – she said. – Reverend Simpson has been there. He knows. Don't believe he is not working for you. Put your spirit in another's hands and you hold him back. – And with that she left, her head straight in the air and her heavy feet beating into the earth as usual.

Ole African had made himself a house on the outskirts of Grove Town. He had found himself two parallel rows of four cane-roots on the nearby property and had twisted them into a shelter. He was resting when the tap, tap, tap of Dan's code came through to him. It was dusk and the Reverend Simpson had returned tired from a day of visiting. He settled himself in the old rocking-chair and let his mind move where it would to deal with what issue it would. It went to the cane-piece on the outskirts of Grove Town, to the man with the dirty tattered skirt and the leather strips for hair, to talk of things ancient and modern.

      – Willie, I've got our message, – Dan said.

      – Yeah – said Willie.

      – Yeah – said Dan – "The half has never been told". There is more of the dratted thing to come. But us Willie, us. What a clear clean sound: "the half has never been told"? –

– Yeah – said Willie.
– Yeah – said Dan. – Now if the half has never been told, you must know what has been told and have some wind of what has not been told. –
– Yeah – said Willie.
– Well, tell man tell – said Dan.
– How come we've never won? – said Willie.
– Yeah man, yeah – said Dan, waiting.
– Oh yeah – said Willie. – They stole our sound. –
– Yeah, yeah – said Dan, still waiting.
– We got no support man. No one could hear us. –
– Yeah? – asked Dan, thinking.
– Yeah – said Willie. – They sold Joseph, my man. –
– Yeah, yeah, yeah – said Dan, still thinking.
– Conjure men, voodoo men, wizards and priests. They didn't like us man. –
– Yeah – said Dan, now seeing the light.
– Yeah – said Willie – they gave them our voice. –
– Yeah – said Dan, enlightened now – they sent in their message, using our voice. –
– Yeah – said Willie.
– They sold Joseph in Egypt – said Dan. – Hoodoo men, voodoo men gave them our sound. –
– Yeah my spar. We said men should keep and learn to use their power. –
– "For God has not given us the spirit of fear but of power and love and of sound mind." Second Timothy one, verse seven. –
– They said men should give them that power. –
– In exchange for fear, yeah, yeah, yeah. –
– "Easier to rule", they said. –
– Then came the outers singing our song, ruling the rulers. Hoodoo men, voodoo men, wizards and priests. Gave them our sound, then sold their own souls. –
– Easier to rule? Ha! Easier to follow. Easier to be a zombie. No faith in the people, no faith in themselves. They didn't like us man. We said folks should keep their . . . –
– Power. –

– They split man from his self. A working zombie. –
– Split them from us. Made us a joke. Made us a blot. –
– And "those tacky old ships". Remember that Dan? Six
  hundred years ago, five hundred years ago, four
  hundred years ago and here in those 1760's: "We'll
  quiet them and send them back to their tacky old
  ships". Remember? –
– Can I forget? –
– They sold out our sound. –
– Yeah – said Dan.
– Learnt our tune from the brethren. On the inside. –
– They sold Joseph, Dan. –
– Now the half has been told brother — said Dan,
  reining in his anger. – Where is the other? –
– Planning a strategy, mate. –
– Planning a strategy? –
– Yeah. Planning a strategy. To beat back those spirit
  thieves and make our way home. –
– To beat back those spirit thieves and make our way
  home? –
– Them tacky ships have dropped their sails and turned
  to steam; have dropped their ships and turned to
  books. –
– So what do you know brother? – asked Dan.
– Joseph went back. –
– His bones my brother. –
– What better, mate? – asked Willie. – But first he was
  the head man in Egypt. –
– And how! –
– Get in their books and know their truth, then turn
  around ship and books into those seven miles of the
  Black Star line so desperately needed and take who
  will with you. –
– Me man? – asked Dan.
– You man – countered Willie.
– Then what's this with you being in the wilderness and
  not learning their ways – asked Dan. – And Perce? Why
  is he stuck in some grove talking to snails and me
  alone in this Egypt? –
– Some have to root, man – said Willie.

– Run that my way again, mate – begged Dan.
– A terrible likeness, Dan. "A stone escaped. Turned into islands . . ." Perce and I are the hills and the trees. Call us the landscape man, the real estate man. A one must know this land, have this land, work this land before he can walk safely at home. –
– I read you. A practice pitch for those who want to step. –
– Oh yeah. You read me. Step number one. –
– Step number two is me? –
– Well read. You are the smallpox, teacher. You learn the outer's ways, dish it out in little bits, an antidote man, against total absorption. You see their plans clearly, can follow more closely. You see where to put what, to change what. You change those books, you take those ships and away we go. Right? –
– Right. –
– So Dan, you keep on keeping on. Stick with the learning and build who feels they want to be built. –

Willie signed off to finish his sleep. Night was falling and it would soon be time to go into Grove Town for his shut-pan. The Reverend Simpson woke up: "Must learn their ways", he muttered sleepily to himself, "and pass it on, but just enough for an antidote. So this is where the Mistress Maydene comes in!" And he chuckled: "Here come de white hen, Mr. Joe my Daddy-O. And what about the other two ladies?" he continued to himself. He recalled that Willie had said nothing clearly about them. "But they are in it", he thought, "that's why he's made his way from the hills. Must be then that one of them or both will make the team." He was fully awake now. He smiled "Miss Amy and Miss Anita, I will see that you learn how to fight this little spirit thief. Someday maybe, you be strong enough and learn to fight the bigger one." He checked his watch. 7.30 p.m. "That we may be delivered from unreasonable and wicked men; for not all men have faith." Second Thessalonians, chapter three, verse two. You are right Willie. Not all men have faith. Time to prepare myself to pray with them."

Maydene Brassington could not see her time-piece but

thought it must be somewhere near 8 p.m. She ought to be pushing home. William would worry, but first things first. Here was the spirit of the forest with a clear invitation to a meeting. Right there beside the cane-piece in the pasture, with the little girl standing beside her, she knelt to join the prayer group. "Yes I am in", she said to herself, "I have something to give." And she set herself to pulling her forces together to join in the battle.

ELEVEN

Things started from early morning. Who except parson and such business with dates? But Miss Gatha did have her numbers right. It was the 27th. Sunday the 27th of January in fact, and that was when silent Miss Gatha started to talk. Anyone who had never seen Miss Agatha Paisley in the spirit before would think is a coconut tree in a private hurricane that was coming down the road. Or somebody else might say is Birnamwood come to Dunsiname. Miss Gatha looking like she had a warning. The long green dress with the tiny red flowers, the head-tie of the same print tied rabbit-ear fashion, the big wooden circles in her ears and the bunch of oleander gripped tight in her hands like they were one and the same. And the swinging and the swaying and the twirling! Miss Gatha now have no ordinary foot walking thump-thump and mashing the stones down into the mud. Toes only and the legs and thighs are oars.

With her body braced back 45 degrees from the ground, was how Miss Gatha walked that morning through Grove Town. Her ten little black toes, escaping from the long green and red dress, scratched the gravel of the road like a common fowl looking for worms. That was the delicate side of her motion. And then there was the large: still with the back at an angle of 45 degrees to the ground, she took long steps, beginning with and ending with her heel. It was early and the road was empty because it was a Sunday morning. No one was about, fetching wood or water or going to the field. This was the quiet time. Getting in the mood for the Sunday service. Miss Gatha had no audience. But Miss Gatha spoke and that was how her private hurricane became a public event.

The spirit led her to the Baptist manse. Seems the warning was for Reverend Simpson. So Miss Gatha spoke: "Nine times three is twenty-seven. Three times three times three". She recited; she sang; she intoned. In one register, in another; in one octave, then higher. Lyrically, with syncopation, with improvisations far, far out from her original composition. The changes were musical only. The lyrics never changed. "Nine times three is twenty-seven. Three times three times three." And then the wheeling, the turning, the bending, the scratching and the moving on the heels. Reverend Simpson did not even look outside of his window at Miss Gatha. And though the whole concert was a public event by now, it was with the ears and the head that people saw it. They shooed the children back inside and closed the wooden windows facing the road. Miss Gatha dancing. Miss Gatha talking. Miss Gatha warning. Man would feel. And that would be hard enough. Why watch too? Reverend Simpson continued to dress for church. He had to. He was going. But it was going to be a 'Dear Roger' day for him. 'Dear Roger, the scripture moveth me and you in sundry places.' Not a single soul, except perhaps Mass Levi – and he raised his eyebrows to himself – would be in church today. It was Miss Gatha's day. "Bless her soul", he said to himself and again to himself: "There are so many paths . . ."

The spirit moveth too in sundry places. Or perhaps Miss Gatha had called them. For by the time she started her dance back home, visitors had arrived from near and from far and had occupied her tabernacle. They were men and women. All in dresses. White and red were the colours. Some wore a white dress with a red head-tie. Some a red dress with a white head-tie. Some a white dress with a white head-tie. And others a red dress with a red head-tie. The dress styles varied little but the nature of the head-tie, not at all. All with rabbit ears. All with pencils in the head-tie on the right-hand side. All yellow and newly sharpened. Then came the drums, their bum-batti-bum-battie-bum-battie-bum, the next item on the programme of music and recitation, that the Sunday morning offered to Grove Town's people now captives in their own homes. And when the cutting and the clearing was done, and the spirits had recognized each other and Miss Gatha had been let into her tabernacle, singing a hundred times louder than Miss Gatha's had been, began. And the groaning. And the dancing of so many feet, tramping on the listeners' mind.

Miss Gatha's solo had begun about eight o'clock in the

morning. It had caught Mass Levi in the latrine. He never left it. Nine times three is twenty-seven. Three times three times three. If she didn't change her style so much! If she would only keep one tune, he could follow her and hold her. But that woman was slippery. And trying to catch her was taking away from his concentration and he needed all his energy and particularly today since it was Sunday and it was the 27th, three times three times three indeed. Dealing with her drained him. Now the bum-batti-bum-batti-bum-batti-bum, was deafening him. He had to let go of the doll so he could use both his hands to push the sound from his ears. On came the groaning and the stomping, like a hundred men stepping on his chest to cut off his breath and to force him into an asthmatic attack. He pulled his feet up to his chest to protect himself. A baby in the fetal position. His pants half-way down, his BVD grinning, his bottom in the circle of the latrine seat, his privates hanging down like a wet rat and his doll and his books scattered on the floor of the latrine. This was Mass Levi who some time ago had tied a thief to a tree and said "Root". He had not given up though. He was boxing and kicking off those sounds and those feet thumping his chest, with much determination if with little success.

The tabernacle didn't break for Sunday dinner. The drumming, the singing and groaning continued straight through to nightfall. Anita had spent all her fifteen years in Grove Town but she had never before sat in on Miss Gatha's performance, though she had heard things. The Holness' were strangers to the district. They had never seen Miss Gatha operate but they too had heard things. In any case, they had grown up and lived in areas similar to Grove Town so they knew that "three times three times three" and the singing and the drumming and the groaning that held the district frozen in its grip, had meaning. They too closed their doors and windows. Could it be that with the windows closed in the day – for they were always closed at nights – Anita was being oxygen-starved? Five and eight o'clock had not come in that house without the usual occurrence but thanks to continued prayer, it had been less and less dreadful. Miss Gatha's solo had found that house in prayer and they had given thanks that the thing that usually pulled and pushed the two women in the house was barely felt that morning. Why with things going so well, should Anita now be putting her hands up to her ears, complaining that the noise from the tabernacle was "suffocating" her? True the whole situation was packed with awe and dread but it was so for everyone in the house this time and nobody else was taking it as hard as Anita, a child who had gone through so much and conquered. And it must have been bad indeed for her for Teacher Holness just managed to catch her fainting form.

Fainting was one thing. They could fan her and rub her up with smelling salts. And they did. But what to do when the child's face changed to that of an old woman and she began in her stupor to moan and groan like Miss Gatha and her companions at the tabernacle? Where Miss Gatha herself had fallen on the ground; where they had pinned her dress between her legs; where she was thrashing, boxing and kicking and screaming what seemed like "Let me go"; where her face changed to that of a beautiful fifteen-year-old and back again to that of a woman of Miss Gatha's sixty odd years and back again and back again and back again until she was silent, her limbs quiet and she was fifteen years old. In the tabernacle there was no consternation at these changes. There, there was instead joy: "Amen", "Thank the Lord", "Telephone from earth to heaven, telephone". There, water mother, full in white, lifted the whistle from her belt and with its cord still joined to her waistband, moved it to her lips and blew one long, sharp report. All jumping, singing, drumming and groaning ceased and everyone, including water mother herself, froze. She blew again, said softly "It is finished" and with that all took what they had and left Miss Gatha's form with its fifteen-year-old face on the ground.

It wasn't strange that Mass Levi should spend the whole day in the privy. He had given up breakfast and along with it, the company of his wife and young son. He had quite a while now been giving this time to his books, his prayers and the privy. Normally on a Sunday morning though, he would get out and prepare himself for the eleven o'clock service. But even he in his solitary world must hear the singing and the drumming and know that this was a Miss Gatha day and that there would be no church. So it wasn't strange to Miss Iris that he should let eleven o'clock too, find him in the privy. He did usually eat Sunday dinner. But since this was not to be a church day, he could have decided to make it a whole day fast. He had had those too. And since he had stopped speaking to anybody or answering their questions, he could be having a whole day fast right there with his books in the privy without letting on to anyone. Miss Iris was not at that time studying what Mass Levi was doing in the latrine: she was far too vexed for that. She was thinking how unreasonable the man had become. How could he sit there all day and expect his wife and son to do their business in a chamber pot or behind a tree somewhere? It wasn't fair.

It was the young girl's scream in the privy that made her consider what was going on with him. She knew that she distinctly heard a scream and wasn't sure, but she thought she heard the words, "Let me go". She thought too that she had heard scuffling like someone was pulling themselves away and like someone had hit someone down. Those loudmouthed chocolate leaves were in the way. Pulling herself up like a ballet dancer, she tiptoed through them to the side of the latrine and listened. Nothing. But she was quite sure she had heard something. Not even the sound of a man clearing his throat or turning a page now. She listened again and got bold: the man might be sleeping. She would dare. She would peep. But how to get to where the air-vent was. The wash-tub nearby gave her the answer. She tiptoed through the leaves again, helped it up on her head, tiptoed again, turned the tub upon its face and stepped up. It was the dolly baby that struck her most. What Levi make dolly baby for? Miss Iris couldn't imagine her superior husband asking anyone to make a thing like that for him, so he had to have made it himself. And she didn't even know the man could make image! Then she noticed his position. No normal man could sit in that position and so quiet. No normal man wouldn't by now feel somebody staring at him and shift. Something was definitely wrong. She got bolder.

It was still the doll that caused her most consternation when she eventually opened the privy door. The face on the little thing looked exactly like Euphemia's daughter's face. If it was Calvert who had that doll she could understand. She knew how

74

the boy felt about that child. But the father! Could one have had it and the other one have stolen it away? But what would Levi have it for? The question came back: what Levi doing with dolly baby? When she looked closer and saw the circle etched round her head-cup, the knife marks where her legs meet and the bright new nail through her neck, she knew Calvert had nothing to do with that and that this was a very serious matter. She looked at her husband: his fist clenched, his arms crossed at his chest, his knees pulled up, his pants down and his flaccid thing hanging loose, and a whole world of understanding opened up itself to her. He was as dead as dodo but that was only one thing. The other was a serious, serious thing. She closed the door calmly and made for the manse.

If she were to go to the Reverend's house, Jonathan and Louise might be there. With all the strangeness around they might have decided to stay right there at their work-place. If the Reverend were in church, he would be alone because no service had been kept. She wanted no witnesses to what she had to say and if possible no witnesses to her having come to see him. The church it was to be. Reverend Simpson seemed to have been praying. He must have heard the church door open because as she got in through the door, she saw his body rise and turn around. He straightened up and came down the aisle to her with his arms outstretched. He took both her hands, folded them as if for praying, looked into her eyes, gave her no time to make what would have been in any case an incoherent report, just said, "It is finished. Don't touch the Bible. Just pull the knife out of it by the handle and drop it in the pit. Take the other books up one at a time in your left hand. Without looking at what is inside, tear the leaves out. Tear each leaf down, then tear it across, then drop each too in the pit. Bury the covers – the hard parts of the books – then when you have time, dig them up, pour kerosene oil over them and burn them without reading what is written on them." He stopped, looked deep into her eyes, inviting collusion: "Your husband died of a heart attack. Clean him up. I'll be there by the time you've done what I have told you to do." Then he looked at the shocked face and thought it could do with some answers: "You are right. He did think he could use the young girl's spirit to get him back his powers. Yes. There are ways and ways of knowing."

The Reverend Simpson then made for the teacher's cottage. "Miss Gatha can take care of herself" he said to himself as if it had incorrectly crossed his mind that she couldn't and that he should visit her instead. "It is finished" he said to the anxious couple who opened the door to his knock. "Anita will be alright from now on." He couldn't just turn around and leave. He was searching for five minutes of pleasantries before he made his way to Miss Iris when he saw the lumpy white figure coming. The words "Here come the white hen" came to his head sarcastically. Maydene Brassington had as usual an excuse for coming down to Grove Town. Coachman had not been told that taking Ella down on a Sunday evening was now part of his work. It wouldn't do to issue him with this new directive and expect him to comply within hours. Ella was too new to the situation for her to send her down on her own from Morant Bay. So Maydene had to walk her down and as was common knowledge, this would be no burden since Reverend Brassington's wife did like to take walks at dusk. This was the explanation that she would give to anyone who needed to know why she was in Grove Town. She didn't give it now. No-one on that verandah asked, so as was her wont, Maydene Brassington went straight up to the table and dug her sharp knife into the heart of the matter: "Miss Gatha says it is finished".

That morning Mrs. Brassington had seen strangers, now one now another purposefully making their way down along the track that led to Grove Town. They were not walking in a group. They proceeded as if none knew the other or his business. But they shared an obvious common bond: they were strangers to the area yet asked no questions when they reached the fork in the road. Without hesitation, no glance left or right, each pressed on. That was strange. Maydene marked that. And more, each one had a parcel and a drum. It was the drum that interested her most. The features. If there had been just one drum it might have escaped her. But as so many drums passed she was able to remark the features. They looked very much like "magic drums", "speaking drums", "talking drums" – what was their right name? – pictures of which she had seen in a study of African drums in her father's library long, long ago. Then she heard the sounds from Miss Gatha's day. Cook couldn't say if the drums were coming from Grove Town or not, whether there was something special going on there or not that required the presence of those drummers, but the shrug which Maydene knew meant: "why don't you stay in your corner you inquisitive biddy?", told her unequivocally that something was happening. And the sounds continued and she knew that this was an event to which she was called. So off she went with her alibi.

Only Maydene Brassington would have gone straight to Miss Gatha for answers. Like everybody, she knew that Miss Gatha dealt in drums and in spirits. Unlike everybody else, she seemed not to know that spectating around drums and drummers, spirits and spiritualists was out. She took Ella home and made her way to the tabernacle. There, there was silence. Everyone had gone home and there was nothing to observe save Miss Gatha lying on the floor of her workhouse. Like Maydene Brassington, she stepped in. Grove Town would have been surprised to hear Miss Gatha talk to her – hold her eyes and actually tell her: "Go tell them. It is finished. The spirit thief is gone." Maydene did not leave at once. "You will be alright", she said in what was more a statement than a question but whatever it was, it carried concern. Miss Gatha smiled: "You know it". Then she paused and said teasingly, like a man giving his girl her special little name to be used by them only, "White Hen". The spirits had finally acknowledged each other. White Hen became incarnate. Maydene was in seventh heaven. It was from that perch that she addressed the Reverend Simpson and the couple with him on the verandah of the teacher's cottage.

"This white hen is moving fast", the Reverend thought to himself when Maydene blurted out her message. He did not know how to play her. He couldn't figure out how far she had reached. "Miss Gatha has seen fit to recognize her", he thought to himself, "but is she just a messenger or something more?" Her "exit one spirit thief" bowled him for six. "Classified information. A highly trusted messenger at the very least", he said to himself at the same time as the thought,

77

"this woman sure is clumsy", bubbled in his head. "This woman has forced my hand", the thought continued. Then "Clumsy or deliberately clumsy?" Whatever . . . he would now have to trump that card. He gave voice, saying to the Holness': "It is not generally known but Mass Levi has passed on. We are calling it a heart attack. It seems he was not such a good man." They would understand the euphemism. Having spoken, he thought again: "Yes. Knowledge is power. They need that power. They are just about to be ready. They should know." Then he looked at White Hen. "Clumsily right" he said to himself as he nodded in her direction. He smiled and she smiled. She knew he meant: "Master Willie and Mother Hen have acknowledged you. Why should I resist."

TWELVE

Suppose thirteen-year-old Ella had been in Miss Gatha's tabernacle and had seen the yellow pencils on the right-hand side of the white or red rabbit-eared head-tie on so many heads, now up, now down, now moving from side to side, now leaned back at 45 degrees from the ground and without turning left nor right nor up nor down, sailing smooth and slow like the bow of a canoe? Suppose she had seen the red and white dresses full gathered at the waist and a little narrower at the hem, swollen with air, like the Christmas flowers that she used to blow for balloons? Suppose she had heard the ehm, ehm, ehm as the spirit rode and the bum-batti-bum-batti-bum-batti-bum of the drums? Suppose, just suppose, she had seen Miss Gatha on the ground with the face of the fifteen-year-old girl? Selwyn would have been richer. As it was, Ella heard nothing. She had not seen even one of the people with the drum and parcel pass. At the manse she had been given a room and a bed and had been shown how to mitre sheets and was busy mitre-ing. The drumming was faint in Morant Bay. Only those who had those kind of ears or who knew what the drumming could mean, could hear. Ella was none of these. Windows and doors were still closed when Mrs. Brassington was taking her down. If it had been daylight time, Ella might have been curious but it was getting on to dusk and closed doors and windows at that time was normal. Mrs. Brassington mentioned nothing to her nor did her own mother: she had her intended on her mind and any little wondering of that strange kind, was naturally left to be wondered at with him. *Caribbean Nights and Days* on which Ella's husband was working, six years after that Miss Gatha day and nearly a year after he had made Ella the happiest little wife on earth, had to do without that scene.

Eye no see, heart no leap. Selwyn was nonetheless overjoyed. That which Ella had given him was for him purest gold. He had only to refine it. He was going to put on the

79

biggest coon show ever. He was going to travel west with it. And there were the movies. Somebody sure would back it. Father could. Or could get someone to. Selwyn felt himself settling down at last. The proper suit, the proper colour, the proper cut at last. He was about to be ready to take his place on the wall beside his father and his grandfather. The one who expanded the Langley Complex to include movies and picture houses. Who would be on that wall beside him? And when he found himself asking that question Selwyn knew that even he knew that one could take a joke too far. Ella was a dear. She had given and was giving all she had but he would want more. In-laws with real pedigree for instance, who could appear in the flesh. It was for him a sobering thought that he was still at the play-writing stage. But a serious man had to take thought for the morrow. Selwyn took thought: he and prophylactics became the best of friends, never to be parted and he felt himself to be at other times, Oonan's own personal self. Then there were times when he played the monk.

With her hymen and a couple of months of marriage gone, there was a clean, clear passage from Ella's head through her middle and right down to outside. Poisons drained out of her body. When she flexed her big toe, she could feel the muscles in her head react. Her parts were at one with each other. And even her mind came into the act. It was now struggling for a balance with her body. For years there had been something like gauze in her head where she supposed her mind to be. It stretched flat across her head, separating one section of her mind from the other – the top of the head from the bottom of the head. In there were Peter Pan and Lucy Gray and Dairy Maid and at one time Selwyn – the top section. At the bottom were Mammy Mary and them Grove Town people. She knew they were there but if she ever tried to touch them or to talk to them, the gauze barrier would push back her hand or her thoughts. She first noticed the draining when Selwyn started to come around and most noticeably when he held her hand. The gauze barrier was melting. A great big part of it disintegrated altogether during her honeymoon and by now Mammy Mary and them Grove Town people were very clear. Selwyn had somehow managed to push his way in to them and it seemed that Peter and Lucy and Dairy Maid had taken some sort of holiday, or perhaps they had gone away for good since Selwyn paid them no mind, asking no questions about them, though he knew very well that they existed. Ella was a little sad that people who had been so close to her might be feeling unwelcome, but life was now so sweet that she didn't think too hard about them and their absence.

Selwyn had indeed propelled himself through the gauze partition and into Ella's carnate past. After a couple months of marriage there was no gauze at all and Ella seemed to be draining perpetually. And the draining brought clarity so that Ella could, after a time, see not only Mammy Mary and them people clearly but she could see the things around them. She could show him the star-apple tree. A big stout tree with leaves green and shiny on one side and brown on the other. Selwyn learnt that its fruit was a very mean one. Purple and juicy or green, shine and juicy and ready to be eaten it might be, but it would never fall off the tree. You had to climb to get it. If you didn't, it would sit right there and wither on the branch. He saw the banana trees, windmill-like. Big green leaves. Cut one and put it over your head during the rain. It is the best umbrella you could ever get. Bananas, he felt close to. He had lately seen them in the shops and he knew his wife to have come up on a banana boat. She told him too about the coconut trees. He knew them as palms. He knew they grew in Caribbean territory but he knew nothing of their several uses. He knew nothing about coconut milk. He thought that coconut water and coconut milk were one and the same thing and no one ever before told him about their leaves being used to roof houses or their husks being used as brushes to clean floors.

Selwyn's pushing had made a clean passage through which he had fallen into that group of Grove Town people. He was now ordinary people. And more, Ella could touch him. He had taught her to and as a matter of fact, she liked touching him. Perhaps because of this and because he was now with them, it was easy to touch her mother and her new stepfather; to look into Anita's eyes and talk to her; to ask questions of Teacher and Miss Amy. It so happened that with a fuller view of Grove Town and its people, came also a fuller view of her immediate surroundings. She even felt. She felt cold. As she should. There was no heat there in his garret. She got tired. There was washing and cooking and shopping and climbing stairs to be done. And she began to notice that Selwyn no longer asked her questions. He was hardly touching her. She was beginning to feel dry. Over-drained. He was preoccupied, he said. He was casting. There were bits he had to rewrite.

The nearer Selwyn came to being a playwright and a director, the closer came that space on the wall and the question which he was not ready to answer. No one had ever told Ella about prophylactics. Or about Oonan. Or about safe and unsafe days. She knew that if you lived with a man, especially if you were married to him, after about a year of marriage, your stomach should be big and you should be about to bear a child. It bothered her that she was not pregnant. Selwyn was so busy these days, it would really be a company for her if the baby came. But it wouldn't come. Something was wrong. He had said she was a mulatto. Was that it? How could that man enlighten her? He got more and more guilty. He couldn't watch her questioning herself, so he kept further and further away from her. If a passage has been opened in you, if substance had been drained from you, then your body was being purified to prepare you to produce. Selwyn was her architect. If he could not show her how to fill the spaces he had created and give her too, a chance to create, then what was the point of all this draining and changing and losing her friends? Selwyn did not want to answer this question either.

He was busy with *Caribbean Nights and Days*. She would love it, he had said. She would be so pleased to see what had been done with all that had left her body. But she wanted to make something inside, not outside of it. Ella could not be pacified. Selwyn honestly thought that Ella would be honoured by his work and that when she saw it, she would stop harassing herself and him. He had bought her a nice new outfit and she sat among the highest. Not only was she the playwright/director's wife, she was also the woman without-whom-none-of-this-would-have-been-possible. So he told her.

82

She stopped speaking to him the night of her visit to the play. A couple months more and her belly was over-sized. She was carrying the baby Jesus. Then she stopped uttering completely. Stopped doing anything. Even stopped going to the lavatory. Selwyn called the doctor. No. He could not help. He took counsel with Mrs. Burns who got in touch with Reverend Brassington, who told them to arrange to send her home on the earliest transportation. Mrs. Brassington took the boat up. She and Ella were among the passengers when it turned around. Ella was coming back home. "Spirit thievery comes in so many forms", the White Hen said when she managed to piece together the parts of her adopted daughter's story.

Ella had told her stories well and Selwyn had listened well. The breadfruits looked like breadfruits and the breadfruit trees like breadfruit trees. The star-apples were nice shiny balls, some purple, some green. You could eat them. The rose-apples were there, tiny and pale yellow and there were some luscious mangoes. But this Grove Town in which Selwyn set his play, had to be the most fruitful place in the whole world and one which respected no seasons. There were breadfruits at the same time as there were star-apples as there were mangoes. Selwyn knew nothing about Easter as star-apple time; mid-summer for mangoes and the end of summer, the breadfruit season. Nothing at all. It was unnatural and it shook Ella but all her obsessed soul could register was: "Everything is a fruit except me". Months later it was to become: "He has given fruit to everyone except me". Tonight she watched his play. They were all there. Anita, Mammy Mary, Teacher, Miss Amy, Miss Gatha, the Baptist Reverend, Ole African. Everyone of them Grove Town people whom Ella had known was there. Like an old army boot, they were polished, wet, polished again and burnished. The black of their skins shone on stage, relieved only by the white of their eyes and the white of the chalk around their mouths. Everybody's hair was in plaits and stood on end and everybody's clothes were the strips of cloth she had told him Ole African wore. Ella groaned. Where was Mammy Mary's cool tan-tuddy-potato skin? The major character was a white-skinned girl. Ella was the star. He had given her flowing blonde hair. Our heroine was chased by outstretched black hands grabbing at her and sliding, and being forced into somersaults as they missed their target throughout the *Caribbean Nights and Days.* "It didn't go so", she said under her breath. And these were the last words that escaped her lips for sometime. But long conversations between her selves took place in her head. Mostly accusations.

– He took everything I had away. Made what he wanted of it and gave me back nothing. – Selwyn was in the dock. Then the child who had been taught: "Speak the truth and speak it ever/ Cost it what it will/ He who hides the wrong he did/ Does the wrong thing still", turned on her:

– It was you who let him take everything. You gave him everything. – To which she replied in her defence:

– But I didn't even know when I was giving it, that it was mine and my everything, – and then the other got really angry with her:

– How could you not have known? Mule. With blinders on. You wouldn't listen, you wouldn't see. –

Now that – mule – was a bad thing to call Ella at this time and she really got very vexed and set about trying to tear out her hair, a thing she had never done to anybody before much less to one of her own selves.

– Mule? Who you calling mule, you mulatto, – and she pulled at the long straightened hair. Then she was contrite and said to herself:

– I have been bad and from the beginning. I had better pray that the Lord Jesus enter in and cleanse me. – But she wouldn't let him enter in the right form and through the right door. He could only come as the baby Jesus, into her uterus, fully nine months, curled up fetal fashion and ready to be delivered at any time.

Only then did she speak to her husband:

– Mammy Mary's mulatto mule must have maternity wear. – She said it fast:

–MammyMary'smulattomulemusthavematernitywear–
She said it slow:

– Mammy Mary's mulatto mule must have maternity wear. –

She sang it. She said it in paragraphs. She said it forever. Ella had tripped out indeed. Selwyn was scared stiff.

84

THIRTEEN

It was Reverend Brassington who had married Ella's mother to her step-father. The Baptist church was near to them and they loved Reverend Simpson and would have wanted to have been married by him in his church but it would have looked bad. Ella was partly living with the Brassingtons and Mrs. Brassington was coming to the house every week. It would look bad to have a wedding and not ask them to do it. Moreover it was Taylor who really shoed their horse, so it would look double bad. And then the Reverend said that he could not do it unless they started coming to his church at least once a month and then took steps to join his fellowship. Well this would mean going to Morant Bay, the two of them, once a month on a Sunday. That wasn't too bad. Taylor's children did not live with him and there was nobody else, so there was really nothing to keep him in his house and away from church up at Morant Bay. Ella was up there on Sundays and Mary had nobody else but she, so the two of them, she and Taylor wouldn't lose anything to take the walk to Morant Bay once a month. None of them was church-goer but Taylor said it was time for them to settle down in some church. He had thought of Baptist for himself. What was there to stop him going to Baptist still, if he had a mind, though he was in Reverend Brassington's fellowship? People don't run people from church and least of all would Reverend Simpson. So when all was said and done, joining Methodist and getting married in that church in Morant Bay, was really no great hindrance.

And there were sweet sides to this thing. How often Taylor and Mary ever get a chance in their whole life to tidy themselves and walk out together on an evening? So they dress up now and start to walk the three miles to church. Parson seemed pleased enough and then said that they could now come to enquirers' class and after he was satisfied with them, they could get the hand of fellowship and he would post their wedding banns and they could begin to plan their wedding seriously. So now they had to make time not only to come to church on Sunday evening but to come out too on a Wednesday evening to enquirers' class. It was just the two of them and the Reverend in the class. Mary and her intended. They knew that parson had put on this special session just for them since they were going to get married. None of them could afford to not turn up one day. How that would look? So Mary had now to drop off some of her banana carrying in order to find the time. But Taylor said that was alright: might as well get used to not carrying banana for her living for after marriage that would stop.

The Reverend Brassington was thinking that their meeting alone was a good thing. For his own personal reasons. Maydene was going down to this place ever so often and it unsettled him. It was like righting the balance for two of them to be at his place this now and again. From a practical point of view too it was good, for they could drop him some hints if there was any danger to her. Besides that, their child was in his home and if she was to be going back and forth from theirs to his as he had heard Maydene say was the arrangement, then he needed to be in touch with these people to know what was being carried from Grove Town to his table. So Mary and Taylor were really two pawns in the Reverend's struggle with Grove Town. Which is not to say that he was any less aware of them as souls to be converted than he would have been of anyone else who was not related to his adopted daughter and did not come from that dratted place. He was very much aware of them as inquiring individuals. He even told himself that they were born conscious Christians. They were just the two of them waiting for the right hand to lift them up into the fellowship.

Mary and Taylor were not and had not been living together. Parson Brassington knew that. Perhaps they would have if Mary had not gone to Morant Bay and come back with a whiteman's baby in her stomach. Reverend Brassington did not know this and asked no questions which might inform him. He only saw two people – a man and a woman in their early and late 30s from Grove Town who had not been living in sin and wanted to get married. For him this meant a serious effort to keep the laws of God. He did not ask how many children Taylor had nor how many women he had lived with. This Taylor had indeed never lived in sin but his children and therefore his acts of fornication were legion. The Reverend did not ask. The Reverend did not care to know. He could not help knowing about Mary's sin, though. It was now a part of his household. But one could hardly call that a sin. The Reverend had cogitated on this thing many a time. How can a black woman really be Eve when the God of the garden had stacked the cards so that she could not say "No"? As far as the Reverend was concerned Mary was a virgin and so was her fiancé. They were a trying couple, trying to shake off living in the Grove Town style. They were striving to keep Commandment No. 1 in the Reverend's book, on which commandment hung all the laws and the prophets. And this was why he thought it so unfair that Maydene should be trying to get herself involved in watching the exotic and in the process keeping their child exposed to what he was sure they were trying to get themselves and her away from.

When Maydene told him about her encounter with the old ragged necromancer, Reverend Brassington took counsel with himself, decided that he had a moral duty to the betrothed couple and that he would personally get Ella out of Grove Town and away from his wife's studies. Then Maydene told him about the Miss Gatha day and the happenings and that clenched it. The Reverend Brassington was on his way to early service at Yallahs when he met the drummers, their drums and their parcels. He noticed them, took in the meaning and mentally shook his head: "My people. Oh my people. Somewhere that lid is going to fly off and all hell will be let loose." He was coming back to his Sunday dinner when the moaning and the groaning was in full swing. It was faint in Morant Bay but not so much so that the ear accustomed to drums and such, could not hear it. Reverend Brassington knew well about these things. He picked up the sound – Grove Town – and he was sure that he was right about taking Ella completely out of it. Then Maydene added her strangeness to the tale.

Now not just the tale but the teller bothered him. No

longer science but participation. Maydene was trying to explain to him that a new self had been revealed to her at Miss Gatha's tabernacle – she actually said, "tabernacle" – and that she moved a step higher on the verandah of the teacher's cottage in the presence of the Holness' and the Reverend Simpson. It was revealed to her, she was telling him that her name and function were 'White Hen' and that she was and had been working with the Reverend Simpson who was Mr. Dan; that Miss Gatha was Mother Hen and the necromancer, Master Willie; that they had been and were a team. She could not tell him how she came to this understanding or why those names; just that that was so. The funny thing about it, the Reverend thought, is that she is serious. Seems his wife was having an early menopause and that it was affecting her mind. She had always been strange. This walking about at nights. But it was this strangeness that had made her such a dear, made her transportable from the cold damp north to the parched loam of this St. Thomas parish. But this was too much strangeness now. And it was bringing unfairness. It was not fair to Maydene in her condition, to take on the child; it was not fair to the child and her relatives. Ella would have, post haste, to be out of Maydene's influence for the time being.

Maydene's strangeness was concentrated in one area of her life – the spiritual. It showed mainly in her praying. From the night of her meeting with the necromancer, she had taken to praying at five in the mornings and at eight at nights. Now that she was White Hen, she prayed also at noon. But in none of this new understanding of self, was Maydene as wife any different. Maydene was still the commandant in the house. Surplice and cassock, shirt, BVD, appropriate vestments, shoes, everything was laid out as usual for William's wearing and what was to be packed for his journeys was there at the end of the road. Maydene was still ready to be his second at any function he couldn't attend. It was just the White Hen. Since nothing else had changed, William naturally thought that the matter of getting Ella out of the manse would have been handled as all issues had been handled before. William would fake depression. Unsmiling. Sighing. Maydene would ask:

– Something the matter, love? – He would continue to sigh, saying:
– No. But . . . –
– Come on out with it William. There's no problem we've never solved. –
– It really is nothing, Maydene. Something I ought to be able to handle myself. – A bit of silence and some more sighing. Shifting eyes and he would continue:
– Just don't seem to be getting the hang of it. – And she'd push and dig:
– Well let's have it. Begin somewhere and let's see if it will take some shape. –
– Well you might say . . . Yes. It is Ella. You know I've come to know her parents well. –
– Yes, – Maydene pauses for comment, but none comes. – Well, what is it about them William? You are saying that having known them somehow affects your sense of Ella? –
– Yes May. That is what I am saying. –
– Well how does it affect the way you now view Ella? –
– May, – William quicker and with passion. – I am not quite sure we are doing enough for that child. – And before the session was over, Maydene would appear to be urging upon him the view that in the interest of Ella and her parents she ought to leave the manse for training somewhere outside of its reach and that of Grove Town. Maydene would next be busying herself with making the arrangements while her husband said, as if he had nothing to do with the problem and the solution:
– May, you think you are doing the right thing? – And he would put all her old arguments to her:
– Can you stand the parting? You were looking forward so, to having another female around the house and you were enjoying her so. I know that. But do what you wish. – And Maydene would do what he wished.

This time it was different. He sighed. He was withdrawn. He looked under his eyes at her and looked away. But Maydene appeared not to notice him. This really scared the Reverend. Then he took a good straight look at her and saw that his wife was thinking. Her own thoughts. Her spirit was not there at ready waiting to take his orders. Perhaps if he

shook her, he could get the familiar response. Suppose for instance he were to come right out and say:
– Maydene, Ella needs a change. – She would ask him:
– What's really bothering you William? – And she would go at it, fishing the bits out like a doctor carefully cleaning a wound. William did say:
– Maydene, Ella needs a change. – What Maydene said was:
– I agree with you. You have some good contacts in Port Antonio. I think you should explore them. – William knew that she knew what was in his mind. He saw that she had refused the circuitous path this time, had settled the matter summarily and had gone. What could he do? What could he say? He said nothing and he could choose to do nothing too, but what would they converse about later on and how? So he pressed on exploring as she said, his contacts in Port Antonio, telling her all the moves he had made after he had made them. She gave him full secondary support. Ella's uniforms were made; she was taken into Kingston to be fitted out with this and that that women knew about, but Ella's migration from the manse remained a William project.

William did not know what to do with this thinking, praying Maydene who continued to be earth's best wife, but one whose spirit had, as it were, grown a body which was housed like a spare part in the body he knew and which went off from time to time to a convent, or – she said she spoke with others; merciful father! A coven. Thank God for the enquiring couple. Newton James and Mary Riley. Why on earth did people call him Taylor? Whatever . . . they were fascinating. So bright. And especially James. What a grasp of discourse! The man should be a lawyer. Being with Mary and Taylor was as frustrating as it was fascinating for Reverend Brassington. Such minds! But to read the text was sheer pain. They laboured from one word to the next. But where they grasped the meaning, it was a pleasure to see how they mastered the ideas therein. The Reverend took to reading to them. They knew all about the Lord's birth and passion. He didn't need to go through that with them. But they needed to know a bit about St. Paul and from the way their minds worked, it would be a thrill to present the apostle's philosophy to them. He read and discussed with them Paul's discourse on love and his discourse on the functions of the parts of any organism. When they moved from text and argument to application to their lives, goose pimples gathered on William's flesh beneath the yards of cotton that parsons had to wear, and his Maydene floated about his head. How could he but remember his own preparation and the feeling moving between his love and himself, if the man kept calling his fiancée, "May"? It was when they discussed 'faith', that William knew that from wherever he was to find the strength, he would have to have it out with Maydene.

"Faith is the substance of things unseen." He took them back to Jesus, the Christ; to the fact that He had known from way back what would happen; how He had continued to live and work in spite of it; how He had seen His future mental and physical pain so clearly in Gethsemane and had indeed been shaken but strong in His faith that there was another world, had been willing to step up to and through the pain. "We Christians die with the Lord and rise with Him: there is another world, another state, than the one you see around you. We have that faith." Now Maydene flitted all about his head on the hackneyed broom. That is all she was saying: "There is another world besides the one you know. I have been there. I will not deny the fact of my experiences." He had seen her praying. He believed that the Reverend Simpson had been praying too. He did not know what to make of the man whom she said had been trying to use the girl's spirit. He believed that the girl had indeed been ill. Evil spirits do inhabit people and can be cast out. It is there in the works of the Master. The man died and the girl is well. All that is true. But the necromancer and the crazy woman and this business of names . . . White Hen, Dan and what-not. He would speak to Maydene and have her share her head with him. Then he thought as he had never thought before: "Those poor disciples. How did they ever get anybody to believe that the body of our Lord had spirited itself away? My word!"

William remained on the outskirts of things. He did help his wife to pray and a lot of praying was necessary. Her clientele was so large. Most of them did not even know they were her clients but it worked. He saw it working. He did manage to get himself to raise his hat more often to the Reverend Simpson.

He had always had a great deal of respect for him. He had even more now. He had handled the case with diplomacy. There was no scar on his former deacon's memory and the church was still intact. If he was to believe Maydene, he was not just tactful, he was a very evolved spirit. Well. He did not know. He was not saying yes or no to that. He was only still saying that the man was too hard for him to take. Miss Gatha fascinated him and he was beginning to feel her smile. The ragged necromancer, Master Willie, who from Maydene's description seemed to like filth, he had not seen and he hoped to keep things that way. Between Maydene and himself there was a truce. A new understanding really and he liked it. Strange where it manifested itself! And his whole body broke out into smiles. Fortunately they had just about got the hang of dealing with their new personalities when the burden came. It was undoubtedly his. There was no question about that. It was Maydene who volunteered to go to collect Ella. He was quite prepared to go himself. But it was true as she pointed out to him, that the matter appeared to have some aspects to it which needed a female touch.

White Hen lifted her more than sufficient rear. She stretched her neck to the longest, looked here and there. She even went to see the play. *Caribbean Nights and Days* was good theatre. It was coon at its best. She spoke to her son-in-law. He intended to immortalize it into film. He of course was a man on the make, a man of success who could not now be stopped: Ella's spirit and with it that of Grove Town would be locked into celluloid for the world to see for ages on end. There was no immediate way to fight that. She had best turn her mind to what she came about. Her daughter was swollen, the young man said she was not pregnant; he had not touched her in that way for quite a while. In any case the swelling was a sudden thing. The doctors said they couldn't help. White Hen saw that this was no ordinary case. She needed help. They came.

> Willie: It has a head but does not nod.
> Mother Hen: Hair but it does not brush it.
> Dan: Throat but it does not drink.
> Willie: Arms but it does not lift.
> Mother Hen: Legs but it does not kick.
> Dan: It is a doll.

They were teasing her. It had been a doll in those long long ago days, found in Mr. Joe's yard where they all lived then. It was coming back to White Hen. "There was another there too", she was thinking, when Mr. Dan said:

– Yes. It is time to call in Percy – "Yes, Percy, the chick." White Hen remembered.

Mass Cyrus said to bring the child down. He would see what he could do. His only stipulation was that the father and the brothers if they were there would have to come too. He explained:

– Curing the body is nothing. Touching the peace of those she must touch and those who must touch her is the hard part. The family will have to come too. – The boys were home. Maydene did not mind their going at all. And William she knew would go. But would he kick at having the boys go too? She left that as she had been doing so many other things these days with:

"But that is William's affair. He has to manage." And he did manage.

FOURTEEN

Cook say it was like twenty thousand dead bull frog, the scent that escape from that chile's body. That had to be the hand of man, Cook say to herself. Then what come out of her! Colour grey, Cook say. Cook say she marvel that a body coulda hold so much stuff. Coulda stand pon it spy Cuba, Cook say. And she ask herself what that poor little chile coulda do anybody, fi mek dem do her so. Sorry fi her so til! Couldn't keep it to herself. She had was to turn to Miss Maydene and put the question to her: "What poor Ella coulda do anybody, that them fix her that way?" The lady turn to her and say, "Is not all the time is somebody do something; sometimes is you do you own self something." Only that. Woman usual fi fast into everybody business but ask her about her own . . . cananapoo. But the man and the two boy children – yu shoulda see them! Jump round well, Cook say. Say if she didn't know what she know, she woulda say the child belongs to the man, the way him look after her. Den she so favour him again! Same kind of colour. Same kind of hair.

Reverend William Brassington was well beyond wondering what the old hermit had done. Maydene had said that the doctors in America had despaired of her – quite reasonable: black boil or worms . . . what else could it be?, was a tropical problem – and that she should be taken to this Cyrus person. In the state in which he had been, he would have done anything that anybody told him to do, so long as it promised a cure. They had said the boys should go, so the boys had gone with him. He did wonder as he made his way along the narrow track, his jacket entangled now and again with prickly tree limbs, about Saul and the witch of Endor, but it made no difference. He was promised a cure. He went on. And he had come back through that strange country feeling quite normal. The only striking thing was the hermit himself. It was strange enough for one to live among trees. But how does that one get so worldly that he takes pay for his cures in land? And the cure? Obviously a herb cure. There was nothing unorthodox about that. The science of homeopathy was an old one. He did credit the herbalist though with a thorough understanding of his craft. Whatever herbs he had combined had worked well and within the time specified. What a stink it had been! And the flatulence. Like the sound of an everlasting foghorn. Had argued with the man. Tried to get him to some theory of causation. If not black boil or worms, what? But no go. No response. Fellow just simply refused to talk. Certainly an unusual chap.

His parishioners and their attempts at reaching him made William Brassington smile to himself:

"So Parson you start keep cow now. Bet you lose one and don't know. Drop a sink hole and dead. We smell the smell Parson. Or coulda hang Parson, for we hear a sound, Parson. Like the last trumpet, Parson. I frighten so till! But I say it must be a cow a hang or a suffocate in a hole. Come from over your way. Is what Parson?" Or

"Parson favour like school latrine want fix. The smell take over the whole place. And a sound come with it, Parson, all now we can't fathom it." The Reverend smiled to himself: "Like when backra take salt physic." He was remembering words from his own childhood. He was remembering what was said to be 'Like when backra take salt physic'.

"What a problem", he thought. "Some one of them must have wished he could say: – 'Parson, somebody over your yard take salt physic?' but didn't know how to cut through the rituals that they had imposed upon themselves. Or perhaps they don't classify me and my house as backra." And he chuckled to himself. Pass their dilemma of communication, for he knew that they all knew about Ella's illness and had some hypothesis that the smell and the sound were related to her, yet couldn't ask, "How is Ella?" He was on to something else. He saw several backras in houses on the hills. He saw the folk – black, slave perhaps, – living huddled together in the valley surrounded by backras' big houses on the hills. He thought of the rich foods backra ate. He thought of those backras with their stomachs stuck full, tumblers in each chubby right hand all taking salt physic at the same time. Then the sound and the smell. Like a mini-armageddon. He laughed so hard, he had to get off his horse and lean himself up on a tree trunk.

"That's something", he said, wiping the tears of laughter from his eyes. "And Ella is better."

She had studied. She had gone to far places. She had something to give. They had contacts. So they found her a job. Ella would help to teach A class children and would help upper division with sewing. She wasn't taking a job out of anybody's mouth. Teacher Holness had not managed to get anybody to give him an extra member of staff all these years though he had tried one thing and the other. Amy had said not to worry and kept saying it even when she had passed over the river, and he had stopped worrying. So it didn't matter to him much now who did what or how or why. It was alright by him. They had helped to get Anita into training college and that was good. Now they wanted something for Ella. That was good too. He didn't mind at all. There must be a lot she could teach everyone and besides that they were now going to take steps to get the school a higher rating for without that they couldn't get the additional post for Ella to occupy. A higher grade for the school was what he had been hoping for all the time. God did have strange ways of working his purpose out, as Amy had said. What else was there to do but to give thanks? So Ella found herself under the almond tree in Grove Town school yard with forty seven-year-old boys and girls in their chambray uniforms, their feet greased with coconut oil and their faces full of eagerness to learn about Percy the chick, Master Willie, Mr. Dan and their peers on Mr. Joe's farm.

It was a year or so before the war that Ella recited. All through the war things happened to her. Now with the end of the war about a year old, Ella came back to Grove Town, the same staring person who had lived there before. Only she was now Miss Ella, the new female school teacher who went to foreign and came back with a bad bad water belly. This time her staring had a clearer pattern. She would do something with every bit of her energy and then pause for some moments of staring. Like there was a conductor in her head – one, two, three, stare; one, two, three, stare. She would make her 'a' at the blackboard with the deepest concentration and then stare outside. Under the almond tree where the reading lessons were, she would take one little one up to her knee, take the pointer finger of the right hand and guide it along the letters and the words as she pronounced them. The whole class would follow, their pointer fingers of their right hands sliding under the words and their voices trying to catch up with Miss Ella. "M-a-s-t-e-r, Master. Master Willie had a roll in the mud. 'How nice,' he said." Then Miss Ella would stare and the whole class of forty children with her. Like Miss Ella was doing, then listening for the earth's response to what she was doing.

Then there was the day when she went back under the almond tree alone and sat there with the book in her lap. That same evening she went to see the Reverend Simpson. She just felt she had to see him, she told him. She didn't like the way Percy and Master Willie were treated by the other animals, she told him.

– Reverend Simpson, have you read this book? –
– Can't say I have Miss Ella. They didn't use it when I was in school, but I have inspected children and heard them read some parts of it – The Reverend said to her.
– They treat them as sub-normals who have no hope of growth, Reverend Simpson –
– And that bothers you? – The Reverend asked.
– Yes. But don't ask me why because I don't know –
– Yet – he added for her.

The interview seemed to be at an end. The Reverend was eager to put her through the door but she wouldn't budge.
– Something else? – he asked, as if in the hope that his question would spur her thoughts to words. But the time for the stare had come and there was nothing he could do but wait. Finally the words came:
– Yesterday a certain message was being sent around the farm from mouth to mouth and from ear to ear with the injunction, "Don't tell Percy and Master Willie for they are bad, bad, bad." You haven't read the book, so you wouldn't know that the actual message is never told. There are dots where the message should be. But Reverend Simpson, these little children whom I teach, who have never been to school before, all know what the message is. Along with everyone else on Mr. Joe's farm, these children know. They know to besides that they should not tell Percy and Master Willie for they are bad, bad, bad. – She stared. He waited.
– The children are invited into complicity – she continued. The Reverend felt like having her tell him what was the message but

97

that was not her point. Moreover if he were to ask her that, he would set her off on another set of staring and he really wanted her to say her piece and leave. So he said what he had said before, this time, as a statement rather than a question:
– And you still don't know why it bothers you. – The staring was about to set in again. He stood up, stepped over to her, held her by her hand and made her get to her feet with:
– That's a most extra-ordinary observation you have made. Think on it and get right back to me – He saw her to the door, watched her go down the steps then closed the door.

He was like a man dying to pee. Who couldn't get his fly open fast enough. Like a dog scenting a precious find, not knowing whether to bark or to whine, to stand still or to rush about or in which direction to stretch his neck. This one jumped up and down and spun around, shuffled around several times and then fell to his chair kicking his feet in the air and calling:
– Percy, Willie, she is thinking. Did you hear her? – Then he sniffed the air and jumped around some more, muttering behind clenched teeth.
– There is hope. There is hope. There is hope. Willie, my job can be done. –
– Calm youself, Dan – Willie said.
– But Willie, – Dan said – you heard her. How can I be calm? Has she not seen two things in one? The two first principles of spirit thievery – let them feel that there is nowhere for them to grow to. Stunt them. Percy and Master Willie are stunted. Let them see their brightest ones as the dumbest ever. Alienate them. Percy and Master Willie must be separated, he made to play . . . –
– The coon, buffoon – Percy came in. Perce the kind, lit in.
– And where is that little cat choked on foreign? – Dan was happy. He just watched him with a smile on his face. The man understood.
– Where? Where? Where? – Percy continued in high humour, giving Dan five – The antidote, man – he said, jerking his beak towards Dan. Who stretched his neck at Willie, for it was really his idea. Then they both sang: "The antidote, the antidote, White Hen has made a chick chick chick." But Dan it was who stayed in the firing line. Perce was so kind. He acknowledged

that. He turned himself around, bowed to Dan, did a bit of chicken scratch and sang:

"And they never knew that you did it. Roll on my Dan, Right on my man. Chick, Chick, Chick, Congo deh."

A couple months later, he rang them up in his usual excited way. They heard:

– Pinya, the hawk is coming down. Pinya, the hawk is coming down – And they saw him in his black robe jumping up into the sky, spinning in the air and landing on his feet like a school girl playing the hawk, a line of her mates, zig-zagged before her, the hen protecting her many chicks. They watched as he continued the drama in words and action. He jumped, he spun, he scratched as if trying to find his bone. He bent his back and looked this way and that, peering around the column to find the most precious of the chicks. They were accustomed to Dan's histrionics, so they waited. "This is going to be good" thought Mother Hen and White Hen so they took time off, Maydene from cleaning her silver and Miss Gatha from hoe-ing her field, to watch Dan and to listen to his communication.

– And I want a chick, and I can't get a chick – Then he was jumping and spinning again.

– Pinya, the hawk is coming down. And I want a chick and I must get a chick. That brown-skinned chick, that fat, fat chick. Pinya, the hawk is coming down. – Just then Maydene chirped in, with her usual clumsy impatience:

– So she did come to you after all. –

The Reverend Simpson did not answer her question. He only cut his eye at her. But he had to ground himself and get on with the message. He came down slowly:

– Whitehall, England here I come. – Then he told them of his last encounter with Ella.

Saturdays was when Ella made up her scheme for the coming week. Teacher Holness had taught her how. Write out first of all the subject to be dealt with – Reading. Write out the heading of the lesson, the page in the book and the name of the book. Then write out the major points in the lesson which you want your children to grasp. Next write out the method by which you intend to get the children to grasp these points. To complete a scheme naturally required that the lesson in the book be read before hand. So Ella was reading. The lesson described the strike on Mr. Joe's farm. Miss Peg, the donkey was tired of being ridden without being asked her permission; Mrs. Cuddy resented having her milk taken away from her: she would have preferred to have given it to her calf. Mother Hen and White Hen felt the same kind of resentment at their highhanded alienation from what was their own. Nobody asked them whether they wished to sit on their eggs and produce more chicks. Instead, their eggs were summarily taken away and eaten by Mr. Joe and Benjie and those others in his house who walked upright and on two feet. These ladies had been vexed for a long time.

Mr. Grumps, the goat with the dread-dread chin had been grumbling since day one. His first objection had been to being tethered and he had complained about this day in and day out with his "Ma-ay, Ma-ay, Ma-ay". Neighbours had in turn complained and Mr. Joe, to reduce the nuisance level, sometimes let him loose and sometimes tethered him. His more deep-seated resentment was this: that he with his marvellous beard and his baritone voice, both of which he had assiduously cultivated, could be called upon when Mr. Joe saw fit, to jump a she. What was this? He grumbled continually and was of such everlasting bad humour that not even the animal world, much less the human, would befriend him. Master Willie did not want to be bathed. His business, as he saw it, was to clean the earth and where did bathing come into that? But he only said this to Percy. No one would know that this was a being with a grouse: he was always laughing, running around and performing all kind of antics – the very clown.

Percy, the chick and Mr. Dan, the frisky mongrel clowned around with him. They couldn't see what else there was for them to do. Percy knew no father. Mother Hen, his mother, from whom he should learn, was busily laying and hatching eggs and cleaning her children. He couldn't lay eggs; he couldn't hatch them; he had no children to clean. What was there for him to do? What was there for a growing cockerel to do? There was some vague notion in his head somewhere that he ought to be protecting something, crowing about something. But what? Mr. Joe and Benjie were doing a fine job of watching; Mother Hen, his mother and the chicks his sibs, weren't crying for his protection, so what was there to do? Same sort of thing with Mr. Dan. He knew he should be watching. But what was there to watch? Mr. Joe and Benjie seemed to be doing alright, so he just played the fool all day, stealing Benjie's shoes, hiding them and running around with Percy and Master Willie. But somewhere somehow, this lot felt that Mr. Joe and Benjie had consigned them to idleness and they resented it. So everybody had their grouse. There was no mutiny on that bounty though so Mr. Joe did not even know that all was not peace and love on that little farm. Then one day Miss Peg said "I am tired and what is more, I am tired of being tired from going places nobody even asks me if I would like to go." And looking neither right nor left she just walked straight through the gate which Benjie had somehow managed to leave open. And the others, with their own deep-seated vexations, unexpressed, followed. For once Mr. Grumps smiled and joined the group. Ella smiled too. Then she read on.

Hardly a week had passed before they started coming back. Ella was livid. Benjie had offered, when he finally noted the exodus, to search for them and bring them home. After all it was his carelessness. And farm animals were so dear. Mr. Joe had then lifted his hat, and had scratched his head. He looked so downcast, Benjie could beat himself.

– I miss them, – he had told Benjie, as if he didn't know. – It is lonely without them – He had sat himself on a log and had shaken his head. Poor Mr. Joe. An underline without its words! Benjie felt like the dirtiest little bit of foot cloth there ever was.

– No – he said – They will come back. They will need corn and grass. And look at the sheds and coops I have built them. My birds won't nest upon a tree for long, and can you see Mrs. Cuddy and Miss Peg sleeping in the dew for more than a week? Someone might steal them, yes. There is that danger. But they would find their way back here. Nobody else will care for them the way I do. They'll soon know that and be back with me. –

Ella was seething. "The effrontery", she said, so loud that those around asked what that lesson was all about. But Mr. Joe had been right.

Life was happy for a while. They laughed and talked, told stories and asked each other what had kept them from leaving before. No one could imagine what. A niche outside had proved so easy to find and each one had found one. Independence was sweet. Miss Peg and Mrs. Cuddy had found a green field and they had grazed and grazed to their heart's content. But one day their peers saw them running towards them followed by a man with a stick. Percy and Master Willie laughed. How funny to see those dignified ladies running. Miss Peg and Mrs. Cuddy were getting young again. There was hope. They might even learn to laugh. And what fun that would really be. But Miss Peg and Mrs. Cuddy saw no humour in it. They hung their heads in shame all day and neither braying nor mooing was heard. Depressed, ashamed. Fancy being taken for thieves! It simply had not struck them before that all grass was not just everybody's grass.

Loss of innocence came to all though not as dramatically. White Hen and Mother Hen had never learnt to scratch for and eat worms so that though there was food all around them, they didn't eat. Corn and coconut cut up, shelled and grated was their accustom-ment and enough was in their craw to see them through three days but when the three days were done, they too began to feel with Miss Peg and Mrs. Cuddy. Theirs was not the silent depression. Theirs was manic. They paced up and down cluck-clucking. The jokers knew when a joke was no longer a joke. How can you tease people who are depressed? So the happy trio too moped. Mr. Grumps kept away from them all: he did not want to feel their negative vibrations, he said. But he found himself, with his refusal to be depressed, as isolated as he had been on Mr. Joe's farm. That depressed him. The spirit of community which he had grown to like was leaving. What was the use of the whole effort then? As suddenly as the thought came to her that she should leave Mr. Joe's farm, and as suddenly as she had indeed left it, so suddenly did Miss Peg leave her exile. For now exodus was exile. She hoisted her head, pulled her teeth back, gave one long bray – hehahehahehahehaheha, – and she left. And the others followed.

Benjie was surprised. Mr. Joe scolded no one. As if guessing Benjie's thoughts, Mr. Joe said:

– They are tired and hungry Benjie. Do what you know you must do. – And Benjie fed them and helped this one to her paddock and that one to her perch and the other to his pen and so on. In no time, life was back on the farm to what it had always been, and no one seemed to remember that there had been an exodus except Ella to whom they gave their depression. The boys were worried that she would sink into a time they did not want to remember. Her reaction was frighteningly inappropriate, they thought. They could not see what there was in that story to put her into a depression. The Reverend Brassington's eyes popped and his mouth began quivering. His wife looked at him and thought "'White Rabbit.' If he should ever come to us, that is probably what he would be." Then she thought again "Not white enough. Mongoose was there. Is he dark red enough?" Then she left him for Ella. In her short stout way, she issued her order:
– Ella, you have until Sunday . . . tomorrow evening to get back to yourself. –

Then she left for the bedroom. The Reverend Brassington followed. His eyes popping and his smile constricted, looking like a rodent indeed – rabbit or mongoose, – he could hardly wait for the closing of the door.
– Maydene, she is bright. How many times have I inspected schools and heard them read that piece and never seen it. She is perceptive May –

His wife looked at him as if to say "And what of it?" He bubbled on:
– Don't you see it Maydene? It is a negative lesson. She has picked up that. I see that May. And now like her, I wouldn't want to teach that lesson –

Maydene pulled the table-cloth and swept all his baubles off with her: – And what would you do on Monday morning William, in a job that people have tried hard to get you, that you are paid to do, with forty little children whose parents have sacrificed to send them out to you to learn? Hm? Tell me that. No. Don't tell me, William, tell Ella – She thought she sounded hard so she began again, slowly, patiently and as engagingly as her matter-of-fact self would let her be:
– I see her point, your point, William. There is a problem. Which has to be solved. Like her, perhaps more than I do, you

feel it. Couldn't you work with her on it and find a way around it – The Reverend Brassington thought a while then something struck him and he asked:

– May, you speak a lot with Simpson. This is the kind of thing that would concern him. Has he ever spoken of this thing to you? –

Maydene did not answer and he went on:

– Would be good to hear what he has to say – Maydene had to lower her face to hide the smile.

FIFTEEN

It was going into mid January and was particularly cold at that time of the evening. Ella in her haste to get out of the house, had neglected to take a shawl. All she had with her were her two long hands and those she now used to wrap her bosom while with her palms she massaged the forearms of those hands. She was going to see the Reverend Simpson. He had seemed eager to put her out the last time she was there but that could be the sermon which he had to write. Perhaps this time it was already written. She hoped it was, for there was no one else to turn to. Mammy Mary and Taylor would definitely not do. They would be frightened. Teacher? He was her boss and to ask him certain questions was to disturb the relationship between them at school. He was definitely out. It had to be the Reverend Simpson whether he liked it or not, for a solution had to come and quickly. Ella did not want to go back to where she had been and all this thinking and no solution could take her there. There was a chance that, on her own, she could do it. That would mean turning the thing over in her mind, rolling it and thinking, rolling it and thinking. It would mean a long journey with much staring and she did not like it one bit to get back home and find people looking furtively at her and worrying that she was getting mad again. That risk she couldn't take. Moreover, where was the time? Aunt Maydene gave her until Sunday. She did rush one so, but there was sense to her harshness. She really had better snap out of it and fast.

Reverend Simpson did not give her time to hem and haw and stare. He asked her right off:
– So Mrs. Ella, – he said, as he sometimes affectionately called her – You have some answers for me. – And they started coming without preamble.
– The major problem is this: there are alternatives. Why are they never presented in this book? Now the strike, Reverend Simpson – And she told him the tale of the strike, because he

105

had said the last time that he had not read the book. – All the animals originally lived without the guidance of man. Why couldn't two hens, a pig, a dog, a cow, a donkey, a goat live in the bushes happily ever after? We have cats in our houses here and we know that they go off on their own every pear season. They live without us, don't they Reverend Simpson? Isn't their natural state to live without a master not of their kind? Then the presentation in this book, is of some unnatural beings, is it not? –

Reverend Simpson put his elbow on the arm of his chair and covered his generous mouth with his fingers:
– And is it because they are presented as un-natural that this work offends you, Miss Ella. Or is there some particular aspect of this un-naturalness that annoys you. Animals don't talk. I don't hear you quarrelling about that. Or are you quarrelling about that too. Let's get things clear. –
– Animals do talk. We just don't understand what they say. That's not my problem. My problem, Reverend Simpson, is that what they have been given to do and say in that book is ignorant. –
– Ignorant, Miss Ella? The best of us are ignorant sometimes and some of us are even ignorant all the time. That's reality too you know –
– But Reverend Simpson, all the animals there are ignorant all the time –
– I see –
– Yes. Why don't we see them sometimes as sensible, which they are indeed at times in real life and sensible, as they have the capacity to be on more occasions than we give them credit for? Or can we not imagine that people who are not us can be sensible? –
– So your problem is with the mind of the writer. – He knew her story, was acquainted with her grief. Her quarrel was also with a specific writer, a man called Selwyn Langley.
– You are right, sir. He has robbed his characters of their possibilities –
– Dismissed the existence within them of that in-born guiding light. –
– And left them to run around like half-wits, doing what the master has in store for them. Percy and Master Willie can only

be bad, bad, bad. He gives them no mind. He has . . . –
– Zombified them. That's the word you need. –
– Meaning –
– Taken their knowledge of their original and natural world
away from them and left them empty shells – duppies,
zombies, living deads capable only of receiving orders from
someone else and carrying them out. –
– Is that what I am to teach these children, Reverend
Simpson? That most of the world is made up of zombies who
cannot think for themselves or take care of themselves but
must be taken care of by Mr. Joe and Benjie? Must my voice
tell that to children who trust me? –

The Reverend Simpson was squeezing his thighs together
in excitement, dying to dash Polonius-style to repeat this
conversation, but he managed to get himself to say in a quiet
voice:
– Now tell me this Mrs. Ella and this is very difficult for me –
And he did look away from her as if it really was so difficult a
thing to say that he could not look her in the eyes:
– Have you been zombified? – He delivered that, then he
pulled himself up, leaned back in his chair, looked squarely
at her and proceeded to twiddle his thumbs. Ella was taken
aback.
– I suppose at some time . . . when I was ill, – But he wasn't
talking about that time, he told her:
– Now listen, – he said to her. – You have a quarrel with the
writer. He wrote, you think without an awareness of certain
things. But does he force you to teach without this awareness?
Need your voice say what his says? – And with that he began
getting up and Ella knew that this was her cue to leave. She
stepped out into the dark cold. She had to finish her scheme.
– Pinya, the hawk is coming down. Pinya, the hawk is coming
down. And I want a chick and I must get a chick. That brown-
haired chick, that long haired chick. Pinya, the hawk is
coming down. –
– We see your point – they said.

Reverend Brassington took an early morning walk on
Monday. He had spent a great deal of Sunday, even while he
was in the pulpit, thinking on the thing: how was he to get

together with Simpson. It came to him that there was nothing
to it but to visit the man. He didn't bite. So he took himself
down to Grove Town, found the man's house, knocked,
entered, was given coffee and moved into the matter:
– I say Simpson, have you heard the term 'zombification'
before? The thing's been going around in my head. You know
how some words can stay with you? – The Reverend Simpson
was slow in answering. Now what was all this about?
– Yes, – he said – a phenomenon common in parts of Africa
and in places like Haiti and Brazil, they tell me. I've not been
to those but I have experienced Africa. People are separated
from the parts of themselves that make them think and they
are left as flesh only. Flesh that takes directions from someone.
The thinking part of them is also used as nefariously . . .
'immorally' might be a better word. Brings to mind the empty
temple into which seven devils worse than baalzebub could
enter. In those societies there are persons trained to do the
separation and insertion. The name under which they go
would be translated as spirit thieves. But what might your
interest in this matter be? – Reverend Brassington was clearing
his head. He had heard this reference to spirit thief tied up
with the parable about baalzebub before. Maydene used to
talk about that a lot.
– Yes – he said vaguely, then with more determination:
– My daughter – and he felt he needed to correct or explain,
– Ella. She's been thinking. She's been places some of us have
never been you know. I mean in her mind. Intellectually. I
think she has been left much richer. But that is beside the
point. Ella was thinking out a matter. I think that was what
she was grappling with. That concept. Zombification. I must
have read of it somewhere. Seems such a familiar word.
Anyhow. I think it would do her good to pursue the point. I
was thinking of some seminars. Give her a wider audience
that can question her and by the questioning bring her ideas
closer to the fore, if you see what I mean. – The Reverend
Simpson's poor heart was thumping to madness. Were they
hearing?
– It would give me the greatest pleasure to participate – he
told his brother preacher.
– It might be well though for you and Ella to work out a

programme. You are close to her. You know what issues and aspects of issues it would be good to discuss. You can count on my fullest support. – When he left, the Reverend Simpson bolted the door. It certainly would not do for the Reverend Brassington to return for whatever reason and find him out of his mind.

He didn't need to call. The air-waves were thick with their buzzing. "That White Hen" Mr. Dan was thinking "really does take the dictum 'the first shall be the last and the last shall be the first' literally. She was the last to be found yet here she is the first to call. What has this bubble-bursting soul to say?" The pin was laced with sarcasm, which was not its normal style. She came through singing – A seminar, a seminar, a most ingenious seminar, – she was singing. – You'll next be seeing Ella's papers at the top of the files at Whitehall with the under secretaries bowing their heads and saying: "Yes, yes, yes. We are spirit thieves. We shouldn't have done it." –

Mr. Dan breathed hard. He was making the effort to remember that White Hen had a purpose. That he tended to be too hasty and that it was her function to cut him down a peg or two. "But does it have to be five or six", he was thinking. He pulled in a breath, let it circulate all over his body, calmed himself and said in measured reasonable tones:
– White Hen, you more than all of us know that that is possible. Papers published in the colonies must be deposited in the British Museum. Whitehall has its spies. It could happen eh! – White Hen scratched around a bit, then settled at rest, her knees bent and her ample frame with wings spread out, balanced itself miraculously on those folded legs. She said nothing more. Just kept glancing from side to side. Mr. Dan continued. She was new. Perhaps she didn't know what he knew!
– But that is not what makes me happy White Hen. Two people understand, White Hen. Two special people. New people. My people have been separated from themselves White Hen, by several means, one of them being the printed word and the ideas it carries. Now we have two people who are about to see through that. And who are these people, White Hen? People who are familiar with the print and the

language of the print. Our people are now beginning to see how it and they themselves, have been used against us. Now, White Hen, now, we have people who can and are willing to correct images from the inside, destroy what should be destroyed, replace it with what it should be replaced and put us back together, give us back ourselves with which to chart our course to go where we want to go. Do you see, White Hen? – She was mid-way between sleep and wake. "This Mr. Dan," she muttered, "one just has to have him talk it out. Emotes too easily. Have to have him talk, so he sees his real reason and his bark gets some bite to it." And she fell sound asleep.

Master Willie had been listening in. Dan caught his eye.

– Your strategy at work Willie. One more step. – Dan said, flattering him and hoping that he would be just a little more lavish in his praise this time. But there was no loudness in his applause. He quoted:

– "But the little coral workers . . ." – a poem about how one little coral on top of one little coral finally made a firm rock. "True, but at a moment like this," Dan was saying to himself, "just a little bit more encouragement was called for. Did one really need to hear now that the awakened consciousness of these new people was just one little coral and what needed to be made was a rock? This work," Mr. Dan continued with his thinking, "is so hard, is so lonely." And he was about to hook his tail between his legs and slink away from that hen and that pig, when he heard Perce tuning up, saw the flowers and the trees in his grove lining up, a chorus of dancers and singers to accompany him. Percy took his trumpet from his lips, wiped it with that big white handkerchief he kept around his neck, smiled his big toothless smile and held his wings out for silence and this is what he said:

– 'Short circuit the whole of creation,' did I say? That little gal's gonna break it up and build it back again, man. – "That's what he liked about Percy," Dan grinned to himself. "The man was full of superlatives. Makes you feel good. Leaves you to trim it down to size." And he jumped up and down in sheer relief.

– My man Perce – and he shook his head from side to side amazed at all that love. – Hi thee hither – There was no need

to say it. Perce was already flying over, his trumpet swinging from his wing:
– Chick a bow, chick a bow, chick a bow wow wow – And did they bark and crow!
– Yeah – said Mother Hen, who rarely ever spoke –

> Different rhymes for different times
> Different styles for different climes
> Someday them rogues in Whitehall
> Be forced to change their tune.

Dan looked her up and down for fully a minute. He did not jump. He did not spin. He did not even wag his tail:
– I love that lady – he said.

Myal spirits

1-4 : They come to Cyrus to heal Ella
5-12 2 Ella's family history
13-19 3 Maydene after school meditation
20-27 4 Maydene goes to Amy Holness
28-35 5 Anita; stones in house rented from Levi Clarke
36-41 6 Simpson, colonization. First voices, house exorcised
42-47 7 Langley seduces, then marries Ella. Maydene hears
48-53 8 Back in time: Mary deciding to let Ella go (on weekends) to Brassingtons
  Taylor + Mary
54-60 9 Ella's story, then her story interests Langley. Anita still haunted, even at Holness'
61-69 10
70-78 11
79-84 12
85-93 13
94-104 14
105-111 15

Reverend Simpson (Baptist)   [Dan]
                Musgrave
Teacher Holness (Jacob)
Maydene Brassington
Rev. William Brassington (Methodist) ⎤ 2 boys (15 + 17) in school
                                      ⎦   in England
Amy Holness   — son before Holness, living w/ her parents
Headmaster Holness
Levi Clarke — powerful local man; had a stroke one year earlier
Iris Clarke
Miss Gatha — Kumina tabernacle
Mass Cyrus [Perce]
ole African [Willie]

www.waveland.com

Titles by African & Caribbean Writers

Amadi, *The Concubine*

Andreas, *The Purple Violet of Oshaantu*

Bâ, *So Long a Letter*

Beti, *The Poor Christ of Bomba*

Brodber, *Jane & Louisa Will Soon Come Home*

Brodber, *Myal*

Campbell, *My Children Have Faces*

D'Aguiar, *Feeding the Ghosts*

Edgell, *Beka Lamb*

Emecheta, *Kehinde*

Equiano, *Equiano's Travels*

Head, *The Collector of Treasures and Other Botswana Village Tales*

Head, *Maru*

Head, *A Question of Power*

Head, *When Rain Clouds Gather*

Hodge, *Crick Crack, Monkey*

Kubuitsile, *The Scattering*

La Guma, *In the Fog of the Seasons' End*

Lovelace, *The Wine of Astonishment*

Marechera, *The House of Hunger*

Mofolo, *Chaka*

Ngũgĩ-Mũgo, *The Trial of Dedan Kimathi*

Nwapa, *Efuru*

Oyono, *Houseboy*

Oyono, *The Old Man and the Medal*

p'Bitek, *Song of Lawino & Song of Ocol*

Plaatje, *Mhudi*

Rifaat, *Distant View of a Minaret and Other Short Stories*

Tadjo, *The Shadow of Imana: Travels in the Heart of Rwanda*

Warner-Vieyra, *Juletane*

Morant Bay rebellion (1865)
Kipling 5-6
Freud 19

"a cosmology in which the universe is spiritually interlaced"
Karla Holloway